About the author

Vishal Anand is the author of a bestselling short story collection, *Emotions Unplugged.* His book has not just carved a niche in the readers' hearts, but has also remained popular since its release.

After completing his schooling from Ranchi, he received his undergraduate degree in Computer Engineering from Bharati Vidyapeeth College of Engineering, Pune and his post-graduate degree in Business Economics from Department of Business Economics, Delhi University.

Vishal works with a talent consulting partner to several domestic and international companies. Currently, he lives in Bangalore.

To know more about Vishal, visit www.vishalanand.co.in or email him at connect@vishalanand.co.in.

Praise for Vishal's work

'... real and inspired by people and their experiences.'

– *The Pioneer*

'Numerous emotions make *Emotions Unplugged* a thought provoking journey.'

– *The Asian Age*

'...bring rays of hope, sweetness, positivity and reasons to be together.'

– *Dainik Jagran*

'All stories from Vishal's books are full of emotions.'

– *Dainik Bhaskar*

'Sip it up for an evening of emotions & nostalgia, coupled with a bite of humanity.'

– Indiareads.com

'Very real to life.'

– Anand Neelakantan, bestselling author of *Asura* and *Ajaya* Series

'Vishal's writing touches every heart.'

– Ajay K Pandey, author of bestselling *You are the Best Wife* and *Her Last Wish*

37 + Grace Marks

...because life is beyond numbers!

Vishal Anand

Srishti
PUBLISHERS & DISTRIBUTORS

Srishti Publishers & Distributors
Registered Office: N-16, C.R. Park
New Delhi – 110 019
Corporate Office: 212A, Peacock Lane
Shahpur Jat, New Delhi – 110 049
editorial@srishtipublishers.com

First published by
Srishti Publishers & Distributors in 2017

10 9 8 7 6 5

This is a work of fiction. The characters, places, organisations and events described in this book are either a work of the author's imagination or have been used fictitiously. Any resemblance to people, living or dead, places, events, communities or organisations is purely coincidental.

Printed and bound in India

To my mother, for teaching me
the first few lessons of love.

Acknowledgements

It doesn't really matter how well an individual writes. A successful book is a combined effort, involving a host of people. In particular, I would like to thank:

Priyanka Lal for giving the manuscript structure, substance and sharing her storytelling methodologies. Without her repeated editing, I could not have presented my work as proudly as I do now.

Anurag Mishra, Himani Arya, Hiren Kava, Kota Sandeep and Varsha Vairale – crazy friends who read the first draft of the manuscript and gave their honest comments even at two in the night.

My father Deep, mother Binita, brother Sumit and sister Shruti. Thank you for bearing with me and all my tantrums.

My cousin Devashish and his beautiful wife Rakhi, for letting me use their laptop to complete the last few pages of the manuscript when I had damaged mine.

My friends at BVUCOE – Pushkar, Prakash, Suraj, Neeraj, Namrata, Mayank, Anuj, Atul, Malvika, Rishi, Varun, Sachin and all others for being part of my engineering journey and making it memorable.

Ajay K Pandey, a dear friend, for helping me with this novel to the best of his abilities.

Ashwani Singh and Mayank Barnwal, wonderful friends for making the arrangements for the photo shoot and author photograph at such a short notice.

Ravinder Kaur, for making such a beautiful teaser for promoting the book.

My heartfelt thanks and gratitude to the entire Srishti team, especially Arup Bose for believing in the story and my storytelling abilities. Stuti Sharma and Jayantakumar Bose for their hard work and help in making me reach the readers.

Lastly, you – for holding this book. Thank you!

Prologue

I stood on the cliff. Tiny droplets of water glistened on the green grass that covered the hard black rocks. The city of Pune appeared minuscule. The sprawls looked like ants. The vehicles honked hard, but the distant noise was all I could hear. The sky above was darker than ever. The black clouds appeared as giants, resembling the black pages of my life – ugly and dark. The ground below called out to me. I was sure if I jumped from here, I would have only one destiny. I would end up in *hell*.

I reached the ledge's end. My legs shivered. I knew, one more step and I will be lost forever. But I had no choice. If I lived, I would have to be answerable to the world, to my friends, relatives. If I died, it would be an end to my pathetic life. I was better dead than alive. I was not brave. So if being a coward rid me of all my pains, I was prepared to be one.

The sky thundered. Soon, fat droplets hit my face. I closed my eyes. Streams of water trickled down my ears to reach the hard surface under my feet. A cold breeze chilled my face. I felt cold inside. I was not hurt, neither in pain. I just could not feel, could not think. The incidents that had brought me to this day flashed before my eyes. It was the last day of my engineering…and my life.

The memories erupted from every part of my brain. I was lost.

Let's Begin

It is said, behind every successful man, there is a woman. I have coined something new. Behind every hero, there is a heroine who will knowingly or unknowingly create circumstances that will force a worthless, stupid or even a simple boy towards *'heropanti'*. I'm not sure if you will think of me as a hero, but the story definitely has a heroine. So I better start with her entry.

It was the 18th of September. I sat on the second bench of the second row in my classroom, a huge room allocated to Computer Engineering students. I was with Praneet, the boy from Begusarai who found first spot as a friend in the 'engineering-days' memoir.

The Physics lecture was only halfway through, with Prof Jhon busy imparting her knowledge of Physics. Thoughts of the remaining thirty minutes were making me restless. Why did authorities of this college assign an hour for one lecture?

A sound at the door relieved all the students, pulling me out of my musings. I cannot erase from my memory the voice and the girl to whom it belonged, for as long as I live.

"May I come in, ma'am?" the sweet voice asked.

The professor nodded.

"I am a Computer Engineering student. I could not attend any lectures until now since I had met with an accident. I have the permission to attend lectures from today," the girl explained softly.

The room that was allocated to our course was almost full. Starting with Aarav and Vijay who sat in the first row to Shivam and Shubham on the last bench of the last row, there were just a few vacant seats, mostly uncomfortable ones. And with the din we created, our classroom could challenge a fish market.

Prof Jhon questioned, "Is this the class allotted to you? You can see the strength..."

Before the professor could express her concern, the now attentive students chorused, "Allow her ma'am, please…"

"The poor girl has already missed so many important lectures ma'am, where will she go…."

"She can sit anywhere! Here, she can take my seat…" Shubham sacrificed his coveted last bench, moving to one of the uncomfortable seats. Grudgingly, Shivam followed him.

Similar voices filled the classroom. The newcomer had already won over the crowd, most of them being boys.

I did not believe in love at first sight. But as soon as I saw her, I knew it exists. And her name was different from all the names I had ever heard – Nimisha.

This girl was taller than the other girls in our class, at least five inches taller than the five-footers. I measured her with my eyes. She was fair to the point of being white, with just a touch of pink. I had never seen such stunning blue eyes on Indian girls. They were so deep that I could have happily spent all my life trying to find their depth. Her lips appeared soft, rich pink in color. Nimisha was wearing a half-sleeved shirt with grey and green squares. The sleeves were turned up a couple more times, exposing most of her slender white arms. Blue jeans frayed at the knees gave her a sporty look.

Seeing her delicate frame trying to project a tough image, complete with a black sporty watch and a pair of brown canvas shoes, worked a charm. They made her look different from the most beautiful of girls I had seen, in my so-far-eventless life. In my school days, I was a bookworm…studious, uninitiated towards female of the species created by god.

Nimisha chose a seat. A while later, clang of the bells announced recess. Everyone jumped out of their seat, in a hurry to escape. I too sauntered out of the class, but not before I had taken a long glance at her.

Students trickled in one by one post-recess. I had been among the first ones inside, and I had managed to change my seat. I now occupied the bench behind hers. Praneet entered, his eyes scanning the classroom for me.

"Why are we changing seats?" he inquired.

"We have been occupying the other one for over two months. It's time for change or our butt will get stuck to it," I replied lightly, avoiding his eyes.

"Ass, your butt didn't complain for these months and now they are turning sticky? Let's move to our old seat. It has the perfect view of the outside," he picked my rucksack and started towards our old desk.

"Just for a couple of days. Then I promise we will move." I snatched my rucksack out of his hand, returning it to its initial position.

I turned, and froze. Nimisha had just entered. Praneet eyed me, amazed. Suddenly the scene dawned on him. Nimisha sat right in front of me. I could touch her glossy hair if I moved my fingers.

My mouth worked better, "Hi! I am Viraj," were the first words we shared.

"Hi," she said and smiled.

"You are really late for the course." Yes, she had entered my life so late! "I mean, it's nearly the end of this semester."

"I had met with an accident. I was travelling in an auto. It hit a pothole, and overturned. I hurt my hands, legs... these were horrible months."

She was chattering, but I was not listening to her. My senses had concentrated on her face, her expressions, and her juicy pink lips. Why was she having this effect on me? Only my eyes seemed to work. Was it her breathtaking features? Or the way her eyes looked at me? Was it because of the way her index finger was moving against her lower lip? I wished she'd stop doing that!

My wish was granted as Prof Patil entered the room. Nimisha turned around to face the professor. The rest of the day passed with my eyes exploring her at every chance I got.

Two days later, my visit to Praneet's place left a bitter taste in my mouth.

"I like the new girl in class," he mumbled in the lowest voice he could. "She is the first girl I have ever liked," he threw another bomb.

"Really!" I felt sick with his revelation.

"Yes buddy. I can't tell you how it happened, but I am unable to eat these days. I don't sleep. I lie awake because her face smiles at me. What should I do?"

I felt like catching him by his long hair and repeatedly dunking his head into an overflowing commode until he swore that Nimisha was his sister. The noise from the washroom was inviting, but it was just a thought. After all, he was a good friend of mine. I steered the topic away from Nimisha, though I was really upset with Praneet.

We sat in a room surrounded by giant machines. Their black, blue and yellow colours were the only aspects we were familiar with. We didn't know whether we would ever touch any of them, but still we sat there.

We were there to take the Civil engineering test, for the purpose of which, we were not allowed to sit in our regular classrooms. This place was new to us. There were no chairs, and the stools provided were very short. But like devoted students, we adjusted ourselves on them. Prof Patil stood in front of us.

"The test will have four questions. You can refer to your book for answering, but no discussions. Otherwise I will throw you out," he instructed as he picked up a chalk and started writing on the board.

"Did you bring the Civil engineering book?" I murmured in Punit's ears.

"Nope. What about you?" he replied with another question.

"I stand with you man," I replied and meant it.

Punit, from the capital city of Bihar, had taken some months to bond with me. The bonding took more time than quick fix which fixes stuff, but it was a fix stronger than any of these super-glues. We leave our homes to study at far off places, where there are students from all parts of the country. Yet, we make friends with ones who stay nearest to our hometown.

"So, we will be the only ones to fail…in an open book test," Punit declared.

"Naah! There will be others who join us," I responded, ducking to escape a piece of chalk that was about to hit my forehead.

"You have to spread out in the lab. You two move to that corner. And, the pair there to the other corner," Prof Patil's fingers travelled to various corners of the room in fractions of a second.

Thankfully, Punit and I landed in the same corner of the lab. For the next few minutes, we studied the other students who were busy writing.

"You should have cared to bring your textbook with you," Punit admonished.

"I can advise exactly the same to you," I pointed out.

I looked around, trying to peep into Nimisha's answer sheet. I could manage to see only her, while her answer sheet was beyond my eyes' reach. On concentrating, I saw ant-like figures running on her notebook. She grinned when she noticed me scanning her notebook. She was so sweet. I smiled back.

One of the students, Manan, went to Prof Patil, handed over his answer sheet and moved out of the lab. Punit looked at me once, and then went to the professor.

"Submit your paper first," the professor replied when Punit asked for his permission to go out of the lab.

"Sir, I am not done yet. I have plenty left to write," Punit said sincerely.

"Finish it, and then you can leave."

"It's urgent. Please try to understand," Punit spoke as if he was suffering great discomfort.

"Fine, go! But better be quick," Prof Patil allowed.

Punit sprinted out of the lab. I felt like submitting a blank answer sheet to the professor. He may give a few marks for cleanliness. Sitting alone with nothing to write was killing me. So I got up.

"Sit down. Here's the book," Punit took his seat. He had brought the textbook.

"Where from?" I asked, puzzled.

"Where do you think I went? I borrowed it from Manan."

'Plumbing' was the last word in our first question. So we looked for the term in our book. We couldn't find it, and how could we, when we were opening the book for the first time!

Finally, we managed to find the answer to one question. We copied it as quickly as we could and handed over the answer sheet to the professor. We left the lab, satisfied. At least, we had not submitted a blank paper.

Only Study, No Beauties

Usually when I looked at my study table, I couldn't hold back a grin. I was the proud owner of creaseless books; some of them still not out of the bags they were purchased in. The same sight was a concern now. Only three days were left for our first semester exams and I had not opened most of my textbooks. It was not as if I was ignoring studies completely. I had found out that the previous year, the IT questions had been exceptionally tough. I did keep in touch with the important stuff.

One may make hundreds of friends in a lifetime, but best friends are those who help you in finishing your syllabus just before exams. Well, they try! I shifted to my best friend Punit's place with my Mathematics book.

"I have yet to prepare for the exams. Can you help me?" My eyes were a mine of self-pity. The look would have melted the toughest heart, but not your real friends. They know you better than that.

"Why would you need my help? All the topics are the same as in 10+2," stone-hearted Punit replied with the ease of someone who had spent time with the book and its content, also inferring what the randomness there meant.

"I need help because it is all incomprehensible. Have you seen the thickness of the book?" I spread my thumb and forefinger to as far as they would go.

"The syllabus is there for a reason, and also the previous years' question papers." Punit showed off his superior knowledge.

"The questions in papers! You call them questions. They are puzzles from a brain building gym."

"You should have taken a membership during the preparation leave. Where has your brain been occupied?" Punit grinned.

I guess he was referring to Nimisha. He was not wrong, but I did not wish to put the blame on her delicate shoulders.

"Come with me," Punit turned to Sahil who was near dozing. "Are you coming along?"

Sahil was Punit's roommate, pursuing Electronics engineering in the same college. He wore thick glasses.

Before I joined college, I believed that people who wore thick spectacles were very studious. Meeting Sahil changed my perception. I hardly saw him with books, actually never. Maybe, his hobby to watch porn movies made him wear those.

Sahil jumped out of the bed.

"Where are we going?" I clutched my textbook to my chest. Books are dearer than the best of friends when you're to appear for your exams.

"To the reading hall. You need the right set-up to study," Punit put his hand around my shoulder.

In fifteen minutes, the three of us stood at the entrance of the reading hall. It was a place that allowed minimum possible distraction. It had hundreds of students from different branches. Everyone seemed dedicated to absorb the maximum knowledge he or she could acquire, thus creating an atmosphere of competition.

"I haven't seen such a place to study ever in my life." I was amazed.

"Let's find ourselves a good spot," Punit whispered.

We made our way to a separate chamber on the second floor where on a large table sat a guy wearing thick glasses. His book was opened to the last page. The table had five vacant spots, and the three of us adjusted. I sat beside Punit, staring at the other boy.

I haven't opened my book yet, and there are people who have read it from cover to cover, I frowned at the guy.

"Concentrate on the solved examples which I have marked..." Punit pushed his book towards me.

"Will I pass?" I asked, overwhelmed.

"Of course, it's very easy."

I stared at the Mathematics book. It seemed like a giant, preparing to suck every drop of blood from my body in the days to come.

"I am done," Punit pushed back his chair and stood.

"Revise," I replied.

"Mr Viraj, for your information, it was revision." Sahil's smile was evil.

"The entire syllabus?" I stared at them in astonishment.

"Twice," Sahil stated.

"Then, why did you come to reading hall?"

"Exactly. Let's go out," Sahil suggested.

"Where to now?" I asked tiredly. I was just beginning to get comfortable in the new environment.

"Have you checked out the entire city? We will find some destination, first let's get out of here," Sahil was enthusiastic.

"Fuck off! I just started my studies, and you expect me to venture out on a city tour?" I protested.

"We will return in an hour." Punit really wanted me to come. He looked bored. "We still have two long days for you to use this study hall."

"Can you give me time to finish just two questions?" I clenched my teeth. But the truth was that even my hand and legs were itching. I needed a break.

I skimmed through the two questions and closed the book. "Do you really think the syllabus will be completed in two days?" I needed assurance, and they seemed to be experts.

"Don't think too much. Come with us," Punit said closing his notebook.

"Which place?" I muttered.

"Let's go to Saras Bagh," Punit said and Sahil's face lit up as we climbed down the stairs.

We stood by Punit's bike. Despite being a 150cc Bajaj Pulsar, it sounded like a Royal Enfield, the sound of which lets passers by know about its presence, like a lion. Punit's Pulsar was its howling cousin. It had no brakes, though the disc brake did work sometimes. The horn was melodious, heard only by the rider. The other specifications included a *BR* number plate. No limitations on its use as it had no insurance, PUC or NOC.

"Are you out of your mind? Is this bike even legal? We cannot go on this," I objected.

"You want to return in an hour or not?" Punit raised his eyebrows.

"But, how will three of us manage on a single bike?"

"C'mon dude! It's just a few minutes' play. We will reach there in no time," Sahil thwacked the pillion seat, making a cloud of dust rise.

"If we encounter a policeman on our way…"

"Nothing will happen. Bring along good thought." Punit shook his head.

So I sat on the bike, feeling like mashed potato, sandwiched between two pieces of bread, each pressing me towards the other. Ten minutes were all it took for us to reach Saras Bagh.

Saras Bagh was more like a scene straight out of Hindi movies. Boys accompanied by their girlfriends, holding hands. Girls lay the burden of their head on their boyfriend's shoulder. Some secluded corners had been chosen, some sat under various trees, while others walked slowly, arms wrapped around each other's waist.

"This is why I asked you to get a girlfriend," Punit hit Sahil's back.

"For a girlfriend, you need a girl first," I answered knowledgeably.

"There are seven girls in our class," Punit pointed.

"How many of them are unattached?" Sahil jumped in.

"Whom would you have chosen?" I asked.

"Rashi is good looking. I like Nimisha too," he said and winked.

Sahil nodded.

"*Rascals, she is your sister-in-law. Leave her out of the list,*" I thought, saying aloud, "They are out of reach."

"Sahil has found a girl in his department," Punit ruffled his roommate's hair.

My eyes grew almost twenty times its original size. "Really! Who?" This guy was full of surprises. *If he could find a girlfriend...* my thoughts trailed.

"Nothing like that. We just had a few chats in class." Sahil grinned sheepishly.

"What's her name?" I enquired.

"Saloni. Don't start a rumour like Punit. He is talking nonsense," Sahil exhibited a variety of tones. When he spoke about the girl, he spoke as if crooning to a baby. The moment he spoke about Punit, he sounded like a fishmonger.

I took a deep calming breath.

We circuited the park twice and got irritated with every girl who sat beside a boy. It is really difficult for singles to see happy couples.

"Let's go back now," I said checking my watch.

We came out of the park. I retook my place between the two slices of bread.

I hated sight of couples because I had not found the courage to get close to the girl who was strumming my cords. On top of that, though I had not made my intentions about Nimisha known to anyone, still my head always hit the roof if anyone mentioned her name. My insides screamed at me when I saw her around college, just like that police man was shouting at us right now.

"Stop! Stop it!" he yelled as we zipped past him.

"The policeman is asking us to stop," I informed Punit, who had failed to hear him scream.

"Do I look like a fool to you? Stop the bike for what? He doesn't want to discuss the weather. They want money," Punit accelerated.

"But, they asked us to stop," I tensed.

"Robbing common people is their job," Sahil commented. Then his tone changed, "They are following us," he roared his eyes glued to the speeding policemen.

"What should we do now?" I was sweating.

"Just relax. Don't worry. I know how to fool these thickos. I have done that a lot back home. Time for a race," Punit accelerated further. The bike's speedometer swung towards the upper limit.

The policemen had not given up. We had managed to beat them for three kilometres. Another kilometre and we would reach our campus.

"Shit!" Punit exclaimed as we entered a tunnel before college.

There was hardly any light inside the tunnel. Punit had to slow down and the policemen caught up with us.

"Stop your bike," one said as he grabbed Punit's right hand.

Out of options, Punit stopped his bike.

"Move to that corner," the second policeman shouted.

The first one extracted the bike keys, and dropped it in his jacket's pocket.

"Why didn't you stop when we asked you to?" The pitch was high.

"When did you?" Punit asked softly.

"Sir, he is hard of hearing," Sahil informed innocently.

"Sir, I did feel that someone was calling us from behind. I told him to stop. He said I was imagining things," I joined the conversation.

"Don't you boys try to be over smart. Your license?" the policeman fiddled with his challan pad.

Punit took out license from his wallet and passed it to the policeman. The two studied the license. Then he demanded, "Bike's papers."

Punit passed a thin bundle of papers to him.

"Insurance?" the policeman glared at us, one by one.

"It's under the seat," Punit replied.

"Take it out."

"Sir, keys?" Punit stretched his hands.

"I will open it for you. Which one?" The policeman took out the bunch of keys.

"That one," Punit pointed towards one.

"Are you sure?" The policeman struggled, trying one after another key from the set.

How can a lock be unlocked with a key that is not meant for it? He was trying in vain.

"I think I forgot its key in my room," Punit offered an explanation politely.

"Do you have the NOC of this bike?"

"Yes, I do, but that's under the seat, too."

"Great. How many lies are under that seat? Talpade, challan!" The policeman said to the other one.

"Your address?" Talpade asked, opening the challan book.

"I am from a poor family." The corners of Punit's mouth had turned down, as if weighed down by his poverty.

Punit's dad owns a cinema hall in Rohtas, a district near Patna. He has rented out ten to twelve shops to different shopkeepers in the cinema complex. He has a mansion in Rohtas and a flat at the posh Bailey Road, the most expensive neighbourhood in Patna. Punit's elder brother runs a jewellery shop. And, these were just the declared legal businesses. There were hints of several hidden properties. *If that is called poverty, oh God, make me poor too,* I prayed.

"Kids from poor families don't race with policemen," the policeman's rude voice cut short my prayers.

"Sorry," Punit looked near fake tears.

"Come to court on Wednesday. Say sorry there."

"We have our exam on Wednesday," I reminded.

"Forget about this bike then. You need a new one anyway." He turned to his colleague. "Talpade, take this bike to the station."

"Sir, please," the three of us spoke together.

"Your address?" The policeman's voice rose.

"Room No-2, Park Hotel, behind PICT College," Punit parroted.

"Oh! You live in Anna's hostel," the two policemen nodded at each other. "Ask Anna to get your bike from court."

"What's your dad's name?" Talpade asked.

"Ram Vilas Jaiswal," finally, one truth from Punit. It came out because he wanted to save his ass.

"Your age?"

"18 years."

"Come to court on Wednesday and take your bike." The policeman passed the challan to Punit.

Punit caught the challan in his shaking hand. *Rupees nine hundred and sixty only*, the penalty read.

"We have our exams from Wednesday," Punit whimpered.

"You should have thought about it before the three of you rode on one bike."

"I made a mistake. I won't repeat it." Punit was almost pleading.

"Of course. Everyone stops committing mistakes after paying in court."

"I don't have that much money, sir."

"Ask your dad. Talpade, let us go now," the policeman said, rudely.

"Please," Punit pleaded.

"There is a way. Just pay five hundred rupees and take your bike now." This time, the policeman lowered his voice.

"It's the end of the month. We don't have money even for food," Punit shook his head in dismay.

"Then take it on Wednesday from court."

"Try to understand our condition. We are just students."

"Four hundred. Final!" He extended his hand.

"Sir, it's beyond our means," Punit caught his head in both his hands.

"Two hundred?" The policeman was disgruntled.

"We are students," Punit seemed to be weeping.

"Talpade, take away his bike."

"Sir…"

"Fine, just a hundred rupee note. That's it. Pay us and I will tear your challan. Or, come to court on Wednesday."

"Wait sir," Punit signalled us to move to a corner. We knew that was the rate these days. Rarely the police agreed for a sum below that.

The three of us huddled together and emptied our pockets. Punit offered them a bundle of ten and a few twenty rupee notes.

"Keep it here," one said extending the challan book towards us.

Punit slipped the notes inside it. They closed it and gave the bike's keys to Punit.

"Don't drive with two pillions ever again," the policeman gave his final instructions.

"Never in my life sir," Punit took the keys from his hand.

He started the bike and we rushed towards the college. I turned to look at the policemen.

"Don't look back, you fool," Punit ordered.

"What will they do now? They have already robbed us."

"We paid them eighty rupees only. You rascals keep twenty rupees on you."

"You robbed a policeman!" Sahil was disturbed.

"Weren't they robbing us as well?"

We directly went to the mess. Exhausted with the adventure, we forced a few chapatis into our empty bellies. That was it. In the span of some hours, I had paid penalty for a crime, bribed the keepers of law and robbed traffic policemen who worked really hard to feed their families. The college was teaching me fast, but I am not sure what I was learning.

"No nonsense today. We won't go anywhere and only study for the exam," I announced opening my Mathematics book in the reading hall the next day.

"Okay sir," Punit and Sahil echoed together.

"Psst, look over there!" Punit hissed pointing towards a girl the very next moment.

"Don't be stupid. Close your eyes to distraction," I said, but my eyes shifted towards the girl too.

The girl was in a short pink top and low blue jeans. A gap of exposed skin between the two was making the guys gawk at her.

"She is gorgeous," Punit voiced what we all felt.

"Yeah, she is fabulous," Sahil stabilized his glasses that had slipped down his nose brim.

"I can't read. I need to see her face." Punit was already out of his chair.

"Go!" I dropped my eyes to my books again.

"Sahil, will you come along?"

"You think I will miss a chance," he had agreed even before being asked!

They moved casually. I was fixed to my seat, battling with numbers. But I couldn't hold my ground and followed my two friends.

"Since we are in this reading hall, we must utilize this time. Where else will we find most of our college beauties in one go? Let's inspect the whole hall," Punit suggested.

"Okay," I nodded noncommittally.

I did not know our college had beauty in such numbers. And that most of them came to the reading hall. The task of doing equal justice to all took up the whole day! When we were done, it was a feat. What irked me was that I was left with the mountain, yet to be broken.

"There should be separate reading halls for boys and girls," I concluded.

"What made you say that?" Punit and Sahil stared at me, not liking my words.

"These beautiful girls distract me," I complained.

They burst into laughter.

We chose Punit's place for the last day of preparation.

"A syllabus is like an ocean. At a glance you think it's big but treadable. However, when you actually get into it, you are way out of your depth," I declared, philosophically.

"Did you see the matrix question?" Punit asked me casually.

"Hmm..." I thought I had heard that word.

"They are easy, and carry eight to ten marks. Just solve the ones asked in previous years' question papers," guided Punit.

"Won't it be too less?"

"You don't have much time either."

He had a point.

"My head is going to explode," Sahil banged his book shut.

"I am hungry," Punit announced.

"Let's go out for some refreshments," Sahil suggested.

"Now? It's 3:50 a.m." I shook my head. "Where will you find anything to eat?" I was curious, not sure why.

"We will find something somewhere," Punit said positively.

We were out of the building in no time. The night was dark. The shops had closed for the day. Not a single person could be seen on the road. I believed the only thing we could find to eat at that hour was fresh air.

"Look," Sahil pointed loudly at the Katraj dairy vehicle, passing the nearby shop.

"What is there to see? They don't sell individual milk packets to any buyer, especially at this time of night. They only deliver to shops," I explained to the boy.

"Did I ask you to buy milk from them? Have you got any money?" It was not a question. He seemed to be mocking me.

"No, I didn't bring my wallet with me," I replied.

"How do we go about it?" Punit had full trust in Sahil.

"See that bucket!" Sahil pointed towards a red bucket. "They have put some packets there."

"Do you mean we are going to steal milk? Are you out of your mind?" I was shocked.

"Punit, I am hungry. Are you joining me or do you also belong to the Viraj Gandhi family?" he said, emphasizing on the last few words.

"I am famished. Nothing has entered this tank for the last seven hours," Punit touched his stomach.

"Even I am hungry, but…"

"Keep your 'but' and 'butt' to yourself," Sahil interrupted. "Punit, I will keep watch. Go on!"

"Okay. I am with you guys." A mouse in my stomach squeaked.

"You keep watch then. Signal us if someone is passing by." Commander Sahil was good with strategies.

"He might be a poor seller," I still felt guilty, if only that mouse had not spoken. "A half-litre packet will be enough."

"Anything else, boss?" Punit slowly walked towards the bucket.

My face shuttled from one corner of the lane to the other. All was quiet. No creatures stirred to stop the crime. They returned with bulges under the sleeves of their shirts. They had taken two packets.

"Move fast. Someone will see us," Punit almost jogged towards his flat.

"Fruits, milk or any edibles of hard labour taste sweet," Punit kept his empty glass on the table.

"It would have been sweetest if we got caught." I was still terrified.

"How do you think we will get caught now?" Sahil was studying me with great concentration.

"The shopkeeper might find out."

"He may be busy questioning the Katraj staff about the two undelivered packets. Right Sahil?" Punit smiled.

"I am sleepy," Sahil spread himself on the bed.

"Me too. Turn out the lights," Punit unfolded his sheet.

"I haven't finished the syllabus yet," I looked from one to the other.

"Finish it after exams," Punit said and smiled slyly. "Questions of how many marks do you think you can attempt in the paper?"

"Just sixty-four," I said vaguely.

"Sleep then. You will pass. Get some sleep, or you will doze off in the examination hall," he said as Sahil switched off the light.

Brain Teasing Puzzles

The room was filled with the noise from the buzzing mobile phones.

"It's 9:30," I screamed looking at my phone's screen.

"Hell! We are late. Run!" Punit was scuttling around the room, still rubbing his eyes.

"Uff… I have to go to my flat," I said, disappointed.

"No time for planning. Just run!" Sahil had thrown the door open.

"Meet me at Grahak Peth in thirty minutes," I waved breaking into a jog.

It seemed the entire city had decided to take the road to college. Everyone walked with a book in their hand, and the three of us followed the crowd. Sahil was in conversation with his mom over the phone.

"Close your book now. Less than thirty minutes before you are in the examination hall, you are still struggling with this book," Punit was irritated.

"I have forgotten each and every formula. I need to revise."

"You will do fine, stop worrying," Punit assured me.

At college, students stood in front of a huge board to find out the room allocated to them.

"What the hell? We have to get into this bullshit to find our rooms." Punit's annoyance annoyed me. He was worried about the discomfort due to crowd, and here, my entire paper was at stake.

"Yes, we have to."

"I am not going inside this garbage," Punit sat on the stairs.

Without waiting, I pushed people out of my way, not caring if it was a girl or guy. Anyone who stood between me and the huge board of room numbers was a hurdle which I overcame. It took me two minutes to search for our roll numbers. Everyone around seemed to be shouting, but I didn't bother. I came out of the mayhem. I had two magic numbers with me. I wrote Punit's room number on his palm.

We entered our respective rooms. My heartbeat had started to slow down. Yeah, I was a weird case. Everyone's heart beat increases when they are shit scared, mine nearly stops when I am tensed.

The invigilator entered the room with a big brown sealed envelope in his hand. His portly belly and shiny bald head with a full bow-shaped moustache did nothing to tickle my funny bone. I really must have been tensed because specimens like these always inspire creativity in me.

Soon, we heard a bell ring. He distributed the first question paper.

"*Alas! These questions are a brain teasing puzzle in a troubling quiz competition,*" I tried to make head or tail of the question paper.

I counted marks of the questions that kind of made sense to me.

Well, 4… 6… 8… 8… 7… 5… Oops! That adds to just 38. How am I going to pass?

I counted the numbers again. The sum remained the same. I looked up. Studious Venkat had already picked up pace. Vijay's hands were also scribbling on the blank paper. I needed to start.

In the other room, Sahil was jubilant. He had answers to all the questions in his trousers' various pockets, socks or some other piece of his clothing. Assured everyone was occupied with the questions, the invigilator took his seat.

Sahil pulled out a piece of paper from his left pocket and slid it onto his answer sheet. The solution was worth eight marks. He copied it. Next, his hand made way to his right pocket, another eight marks. Every piece of paper coming out of his clothes added to his total score. Bishnoi Xerox had done a marvelous job, photocopying the pages at 25% of their original size. The remaining answers could not be reached for in an examination hall. He went to the invigilator.

"Sir, washroom," he said.

"How can you think of these places during an exam? Hurry, come soon," the Professor grumbled.

Sahil did not respond. He walked out of the examination room, rushing to the washroom. He checked carefully for anyone. He ventured to the intimate parts of his body.

"Stupid Viraj! He thinks he fools us. Obviously he had photocopies like these," he talked to himself, smiling. "And, that stupid Punit has been solving problems for the past one month. What fools I have for friends!" He swapped the papers in his various pockets.

He threw away inessential papers in the dustbin at the entrance of the washroom.

"Please, may I come in?" he asked for the invigilator's permission.

"Come in, son!" the examiner welcomed him with a smile.

He entered the room and walked to his allocated seat, where his answer sheet and pen lay.

"Come here," the invigilator called him.

He turned to the invigilator.

The invigilator examined him from top to bottom. Sahil stood his ground.

"Do you have chits?"

Sahil did not respond. However, his face was pulled by gravity. He could see a piece of his photocopies lying near the invigilator's chair, and some on his table. The cool breeze from the window had blown his answer sheet to the ground and scattered his reliable chits to every corner of the room.

"Yes sir," Sahil knew there was no way out of this situation.

"Take it out," the invigilator ordered.

Sahil slid his hand into his right pocket. He kept the piece of paper that came out on the table.

"Do you have more?"

He silently slid his hand into his left pocket, another piece on the table.

"Any more?"

Pieces came out of every imaginable and some unimaginable parts of the body.

"*Why do they allot three hours to exams? The paper needs only one-and-a-half hour,*" I gazed at my watch. "*What the hell are they writing in this stupid paper?*"

"Sheet please," someone raised his hand.

"*Am I the only fool in our class? Are there some pretending not to be?*" You're not worried when you don't know answers to few questions in an examination paper. You're worried when others are confidently writing them.

Time seemed to be moving slower and slower. I had nothing more to write. I began copying the questions, and then began guessing the probable steps of solving them. I gave it my best, well, as much as was possible after preparing an entire semester's syllabus in just three days. At last, God showed some pity on my situation and the warning bell tinkled. I turned a few pages and my eyes landed on some numbers that spoke to me. Finally, this dumb person could answer a question. I attacked the question with zeal, but alas! The invigilator snatched away the paper. I sighed in frustration. No extra sheet for me and no extra pain for the examiner checking my answer sheet.

"How was the paper?" was Punit's first query.

"What is the word for worse than worst?"

"How much did you attempt?"

"It adds to 42," I calculated my marks, hoping and praying that the examiner would throw marks at every small step that was correct. "What about you?"

"Mine was good. Attempted near about…" Punit caught my dejected face and stopped. "Let's go to eat."

We walked out of the college campus.

Six hours of sleep and gorging like a pig at dinner was a dismal paper's effect on me. After dinner, I reached Punit's place.

"I need your help with this subject," I told Punit as soon as he opened the door.

"Previous years' question papers. Look up answers for those questions. Every year many of the questions get repeated," Punit repeated his mantra.

I studied the question paper. It contained many two-marks questions. These marks could make me sail through.

"Can you tell me answers to these? If I attempt all questions of two marks, it will add up to forty." I was tackling my first semester with many strategies. If only I had applied as much brain earlier.

"I am feeling hungry again." Sahil stretched his arms leaning on his chair.

"You feel hungry at four in morning every day! Why don't you buy something to eat in the evening?" I reasoned.

"Let's go out, please!" he insisted.

"But we won't steal anything this time," I closed my textbook.

"Okay. We will just look for something to eat. Will that make you happy?"

We walked the empty road. It was a déjà vu of the previous night.

"I would prefer to steal another packet of milk instead of dying of hunger," Sahil announced.

"Let's go to that shop then," Punit took a few moments to agree.

"But..." my first question was just about to begin.

"Please, don't start again. Did we not try to find an open shop? We have to sleep too. It's already late," Sahil interrupted.

I agreed half-heartedly and walked towards the milk parlour. Milk packets were lying in buckets – an easy steal. They seemed to be calling out to people who would appreciate them. Punit stepped near buckets, as I stood watching him.

"Who is there?" a person shouted at Punit as he picked up a packet.

"Run!" Punit and Sahil shouted in unison.

I was quite lucky to be standing at a distance. I ran ahead of the two thieves. An old man followed us. Considering his age, he was quite fast.

"Throw milk packets at him. He won't follow us then," I tried to breathe.

"Don't throw anything, Punit. I am hungrier with all this running. If you do, I will drink your blood!" Sahil threatened turning to look at the old man. "He will tire soon."

The old man finally gave up the chase. He stood in the middle of the road, panting and clutching his stomach. Thieves were back at home and sweetest milk was served in glasses for hungry people.

Here I was. Stealing, two days in a row. The guilt never left me, but I knew I was fast becoming a criminal. No wonder I ended up in jail during the third year. But before I tell you about that, let me tell you that I decided to never steal from that day onward. I even told my friends that the same day.

"We won't do it ever again," I said as I finished my glass.

"Full and final. Let's sleep now," Punit agreed.

"I am not going to sleep. I have much left to go through."

"Even I have unfinished syllabus, but some respected man had said that health is wealth while exams come and go," Sahil smiled.

Punit and Sahil slept in the room. I occupied the living area of the flat. The sleep goddess tempted me, but the fear of failing one more paper kept my eyes open. I didn't sleep, but I could not cross the finish line of the syllabus.

Next morning, we walked to the battleground for another war. I was luckier. I could attempt for a total of sixty-four marks. Punit did better than both of us and Sahil successfully copied from his chits that day.

We continued like this for the next three papers. I didn't sleep the nights before the exams, but slept the entire day after I was done with the paper.

We did not steal any milk. I managed to answer little over fifty percent questions in the last three papers and this was how I tackled my first semester.

True Criminals

Let me jump ahead and tell you about an incident from third year. You might think I had turned into one of those wayward youths who forget their own dreams, or their parents' and become the blight of the society; the ones who pose the maximum threat to a country because they simply don't care about what happens.

Well, it wasn't the case with me, though the trip to the lock-up did happen. It's a moment in my life I am not proud of. Before you think any further, let me tell you the whole incident, then you can judge me.

It was a Friday, I remember. The 12th of October – a ground-breaking, rather ground-shaking day in my life. After that day, I formed a habit… a habit of thinking before taking the smallest action.

The clock showed 11:30 a.m. Rather, half an hour before noon, the hour when my day started those days. We had preparation leave before exams and it was time for some serious studying.

Many kids followed their parents' instructions to sleep early and wake up with the sunrise, to grasp engineering subjects like early birds who get the worm. But things were different with me.

I preferred reading late into the night and going to bed at four or five in the morning. The previous night or morning, it was nearly five when I went to sleep.

The two hands of the clock struggled to meet each other at twelve. I left my bed, and walked into the hall. A newspaper lay on Sahil's bed. Sahil was my roommate in the third year of Engineering, along with my elder brother Shekhar, who was in the seventh semester of Mechanical Engineering that year in the same college.

I picked the newspaper, and settled myself on Sahil's bed.

Suddenly, the ringtone of Sahil's mobile drew my attention. Sleepily he picked up the phone. He dictated the address of the place where we lived to the caller.

"Who was that?" I asked.

"The person from The Vodafone, who has been repeatedly calling me for the photograph," Sahil answered, his eyes still closed as he kept the phone by the pillow.

For the past couple of days, some Vodafone personnel had been calling Sahil, to inform him that "…you haven't submitted your photograph. If you fail to do so, your Vodafone number will be disconnected."

Sahil had visited Vodafone office, but they said that they hadn't called.

Something was fishy. A person coming from Vodafone office, just to collect a photograph?

"They already denied it. Why is he coming now?" I voiced my doubt.

"No idea! He said that he is in Vagishwari campus. He may take ten minutes," Sahil's eyes were still closed.

I started looking for something interesting in the newspaper.

Knock! Knock!

Someone was using all his might to get the door opened.

"That must be the Vodafone guys," I turned the page.

Sahil grabbed his tee and jumped towards the door. Two people dressed in formals stood at the door.

Once the two entered our hall, a third one joined them in seconds. We hadn't noticed him earlier.

Still half dozing, Sahil searched for his photograph.

"Where is the phone?" one of them asked.

Sahil picked up his mobile, grabbed a smiling photo of his from the drawer, and walked towards the men.

The second man snatched the phone from his hand, while the third slapped his sleepy face, hard. "You should be ashamed of yourself. Thief!"

The slap was tight. I could make out imprints of four fingers on Sahil's cheek.

I was shocked. The resounding slap had made Shekhar bhaiya come out of his room too.

The three of us stood in front of the three persons and the silence in the hall was broken by Sahil. "What did I do?"

"How cute, *what did you do,* indeed." The men sneered. "You stole this mobile. Its missing complaint was lodged in our police station and we have been trying to track you for nearly a month now."

"I did not steal anything," Sahil's voice quivered with pain and fear.

"Is this your phone?" the other man asked.

A vision flashed in front of my eyes. It had happened more than a month ago, while I was returning from my college. Since it was a Saturday, a half day, it was an early run homewards.

While I was on my way back, two boys on a CBZ bike overtook me. The bike stopped. One of them got down, still chatting.

I walked on. The biker finally accelerated his bike.

Suddenly, something under the wheels made the bike stagger. The biker stopped, looked down to check for the obstacle, and satisfied it was nothing, he restarted the bike.

I looked and spotted a Samsung mobile. I called out to the biker, "You dropped your mobile!"

The biker did not stop. I picked up the phone and clicked some buttons. It was switched off. I pushed the mobile in my jeans' pocket and walked home.

"This phone is Viraj's, my roommate here. He bought it last month," Sahil's words brought me back to the real world.

"Who is Viraj?" The first man faced me and my brother.

I stated the truth. "I had found this mobile."

"Where? What do you mean by you 'found' this mobile?" One of them shouted at me.

"I found it lying on the road."

"Wow… lucky you. You find things, costly things, lying on the road. Even a brand new mobile!" He mocked me.

"Yes, he got it by the roadside," my brother joined the conversation.

"Don't you dare." He silenced my elder brother. "You will never be able to wiggle out of this. You are all thieves. Come with us to the police station."

I was livid. The man was calling my elder brother a thief right in front of me! I had not stolen the thing. I fully intended to return it to the owner when I found him. I had only kept it in my safe-keeping, better than putting a costly device like that in a 'lost and found' box, I had thought back then. Now my friend, me and most importantly, my sincere brother were being called a thief for my good heartedness! If I had given it to these very policemen on that very day, would they have taken the trouble to find its owner as vigilantly as they were here to accuse us? We were not some cheap thieves. I was just lazy and had not yet got down to look for the owner. I am sure even these policemen would not have been so prompt.

"We are not lying," Shekhar bhaiya said.

"Come to the police station. Give a written statement that you got it on the road."

"Sir, please leave us. I am not well," Shekhar bhaiya sounded tired.

"All thieves get ill with the Police virus."

"Sir, he is not lying. He had an operation last week," I stated.

"Okay. But you two look fine. Come, finish the formalities," the policeman said to Sahil and me.

"Let me change my clothes," I had no choice but to agree.

"White and black stripes will suit you," one of them said, gripping my hand as I walked towards my wardrobe.

Left without choice, we shoved our feet into our sandals. We were allowed only that much time.

The policeman unlocked the door, pulling us by the arms. They walked to the two bikes they had come on.

"I am going with Patil, you take the boys on your bike," one of them said.

When a common man rides with two pillions, these policemen fine them. They make sure the riders' pockets are emptied… but come their turn, and it is absolutely fine to do so.

We began our journey to the police station, so that the real criminals of society could pass judgment about common people's mistakes.

"Was this mobile really found on the road?" The policeman with us asked.

"Yes sir," I repeated the truth.

We made our way towards the Vagishwari police station.

"It was here, when I saw it for the first time," I pointed to the spot as we crossed Punjabi Rasoi, a restaurant.

"If you are speaking the truth, then there is nothing to worry. You can leave within minutes," the policeman assured us.

For the first time since they had entered our flat, I felt relaxed.

Once we reached the police station, we were asked to sit on an old wooden bench. The constables looked at us, as if we were hardened criminals, caught red-handed while murdering a dozen innocent people.

"Patil, bring both the guys to the room," one said to the other.

It was a small room with a tiny window in one corner, and the door just opposite. An old cupboard stood by the door. A table with one chair on one side and two chairs on the other was all the furniture. On the wall behind, a picture of Gandhi ji smiled lovingly.

"Sit," the policeman ordered.

We both sat on the two chairs, facing the single chair of the policeman.

"When did you steal this mobile, Sahil?" The policeman adjusted some papers on the table.

"I didn't," Sahil repeated. "Viraj gave it to me," he pointed towards me.

"So Viraj… you are the thief?" The policeman rested his eyes on me, unblinking.

"Sir, I found it on the road."

"Lucky chap!" he mocked.

I stayed quiet. He looked at Sahil again.

"How much did you pay him for this mobile?"

"I didn't pay any money to him."

"Friendship! It's rightly said, thick as thieves."

"Viraj gave it to me to use as my phone was not working properly," Sahil explained.

"Okay. No money involved. Right?"

"Not a single penny." Sahil shook his head.

The policeman went out, "Patil, did you call the guy who lodged the complaint?"

"Yes, he was in his class. He said he will be here in an hour."

Sahil and I called our parents, explaining the situation. The policeman returned to the room.

"Come out. Saheb wants to see you," he flicked his finger.

The room we were called into was spacious. A fat, lazy looking short officer sat on a chair.

"Sir, these are the mobile thieves."

The policeman was shocked to see two teens.

"What do you do?" he asked us.

"We are students of Vagishwari College of Engineering," Sahil replied.

"Did your parents send you here to steal?"

"We did not steal anything," I repeated defiantly.

"Shut up. A few kicks to the right spot will make you remember the truth," he yelled, unnecessarily.

"The truth shall remain the same, no matter where you hit us," I murmured.

"Take them back. I don't want to be rude with these kids early in the day," he dismissed us.

Shekhar bhaiya came.

"You can't arrest them." Bhaiya was shocked.

"We can do anything. Even things beyond your dreams," the policeman took pleasure in our frustration.

The room was silent for a minute or two.

"Had he stolen it, you could have surely arrested him, following the procedure, but he had found the phone," Bhaiya tried to be brave.

"Why didn't you call the owner?"

"How could we? The mobile was switched off. No battery."

"Really? It recharged magically, just when you wanted to use it."

"No, we bought a charger."

"Smartass…" Bhaiya's mobile rang, interrupting the policeman. Bhaiya left the room.

"Why didn't you report your find to the police?" he asked me.

"A common man prefers not to visit a police station."

"It's your duty!" he reminded us.

"Sir, stealing is a crime. We didn't commit any," I reminded him.

"Using things that are not rightfully yours is also a crime."

"Sorry sir," I lowered my eyes.

"If you go into that room…" The policeman pointed in the direction of another room, "…you will find several bags and suitcases.

Think of the things inside them! We got it from different locations. We did not take it for our personal use."

"*You would have, if you found anything of value*," I said to myself.

"You have committed a crime," he decreed.

A senior from our college entered the room.

"Where are they?" he asked.

"Here," the policeman pointed towards us.

"They are students." The senior's voice was amazed.

"Yes, they are. Do you know them?"

"No, I might have seen them in college though," the senior replied.

"They say they found this mobile on the road," the policeman repeated our story.

"No sir. It was stolen from my brother's place," the senior completely ignored the facts.

"How did they enter your brother's place, if you don't know them?" The policeman questioned him.

"My brother might know them."

"Call him."

"He lives in Sangli. I have informed him. He will be here in a few hours."

"How was his phone lost in Pune, if he lives in Sangli?"

At least these policemen asked rude questions to one and all.

"He was in Pune for a month to try and get admission into Vagishwari College. When he was not able to, he took admission in the Sangli branch."

Shekhar bhaiya entered the room. He saw the new guy.

"He is the one who filed the FIR," the policeman informed as he left the room.

"Okay." Bhaiya and the senior measured each other up.

"Look. You got your mobile, let them go," my brother requested.

"They stole it. They must be punished."

"They did not steal it. He found it lying on the road," my brother sounded tired of repeating the same to everyone.

"Sorry, I can't help them."

"If you don't withdraw your complaint, the case will go to court. They will be taken there. It's a long process. Why don't you let it go?" my brother reasoned.

The senior considered my brother's words, "Let my cousin come. He is the owner. It will be his decision."

Two-three hours had passed. My brother and the senior had left by now. Sahil called his relatives in Pune. The policemen were fast getting restless. One of them came with some papers.

"Give me a few details."

"Yes sir," we said in unison.

"I will start with you," he pointed towards me.

"Your name?"

"Viraj Aron."

"Father's name?"

"Mr Dilip Gupta."

"How is that possible?"

"Sir?" I asked.

"If your father's surname is Gupta, how can you be an Aron?" He was intrigued. I am sure he was smelling a rat. Policemen were an untrusting breed.

"This is what it is," I said.

"In Maharashtra, if my surname is Patil, then my son's surname is bound to be Patil. Isn't it the same all over India?"

"No. It's not necessary."

"Strange." He shrugged.

I could have explained the real reason behind my surname, but I was sure he wouldn't understand.

My father believed that surnames are the name plates of various castes in our society. Castes discriminate one person from another, dividing them into upper and lower castes. He disliked this concept so he gave me a surname which could not separate me, from anyone. People like this policeman found it difficult to understand.

"Do you have any scar or other identification marks on your body?" the policeman asked next.

"No sir."

"Any bone fractured? Damaged?"

"None sir."

"Any teeth broken?'

"No sir. Every broken tooth has been replaced by a new one."

He asked a lot of similar questions. I replied patiently. He was surprised with my fearlessness.

The same questionnaire was repeated for Sahil. He followed my example.

"Who will bail you out if we put you both in jail?" He asked the last question, as he placed the filled forms on the table.

"I don't have anyone here," I said.

"My uncle lives in Aundh. He can do it for me," Sahil said slowly.

"Today is Friday. Tomorrow and day after are holidays. Three nights in jail, at least," the policeman said as if he was reading from a resort brochure.

I didn't understand what was happening, till then. We had been missing an important link.

"Patil, bring Ramanna," the policeman's voice boomed.

A man in a yellow dirty undershirt and a torn blue undergarment was pushed into the room. Patil was given instructions and he began hitting the man with his stick. The stick found its mark on every part of Ramanna's body. He cried out loud, and hauled in pain. The painful cries became longer and louder with every action of Patil's stick.

The first policeman ordered Patil to leave, asking Ramanna, "Are you in pain?"

I did not expect concern from the policeman. If you feel someone's pain, why give it to them in the first place?

"Where is it hurting?" he enquired.

The man looked at the face which showed kindness. His eyes filled with pools of water. He murmured, pointing towards his toes.

The policeman moved his heavy shoes, landing on the very spot Ramanna had pointed out. He howled this time.

"Patil, take him back," he shouted.

The trailer was over. The policeman had shown us what he wanted to.

Sahil was wet with his own sweat, his face pale with fear, fearing the same treatment. The policeman walked out of the room, leaving us alone to ponder over the scenario, but we were still ignorant of the point he was trying to make.

Finally, the mobile owner came. He was a tall, skinny, teenager who seemed to have just finished his school. My brother followed him into the room. The boy looked at both of us then turned to the policeman, "Where is my mobile?"

"Do you know them?" The policeman pointed at us.

"No sir. I haven't seen them ever."

"They say, they found the mobile on the road."

"No sir, they are lying. It was stolen from my friend's place."

"I believe they are lying. What now?" The policeman glared at me.

"The mobile was on the road near Punjabi Rasoi, the restaurant in the market. I don't think you, but someone on a CBZ dropped it in front of the mess," I explained, again.

"Yes... Samir bhaiya had it with him last. He does own a CBZ," he spoke to the policeman. "But he told me that the phone was stolen while he was sleeping in his room."

"I found it on the road. Why don't you call him?" I suggested.

"What's the need? I am happy I got it." He smiled at the policeman.

Someone called the policeman. I got some time with the owner of the mobile.

"Please, take back your complaint and let us go."

"Why didn't you try to return it to me?" he asked defiantly.

"My laziness made me postpone the task to the next day. And now we have come to this." I looked around the police station.

The policeman entered the room again.

"Take your mobile. We need to give these boys special treatment."

"Sir, I want to take back my complaint." The mobile owner had believed me!

"Not possible." The policeman totally ignored him.

"I lodged a complaint, I got the phone back. So I want to withdraw my complaint."

"And what about our efforts? Come out," the policeman said to the mobile owner, as he left his chair and walked towards the door. The teenager followed him.

Half an hour later, no one had come back to the room. We had purposely been left alone to find the missing link, the link that would make those policemen's efforts worthwhile.

"Now what should I do with you guys?" The policeman rubbed his hands as he entered the room.

"Free us," I said in a low voice.

"How can I? The police worked hard for a week to trap you and find that phone. Now we just let you go?" He smirked.

We didn't have an answer. The policeman took a Marathi newspaper that was lying on the table, scribbled on it and moved it towards us. '25000', written in small and dirty handwriting.

We were stunned. The missing link! The M-factor.

"This is too much!" My brother found words.

"Your brother and his close friend here in a lock up, that will be cheaper. No more college to attend. After we report to your principal, you wouldn't need to pay the college fees as well. Cheaper indeed," the man in uniform scratched the amount from the newspaper.

My brother struggled with words, "Sir, we are students. Where will we get that kind of money from?"

"Take your time. Until you arrange it, these two will be our guests."

My brother had no choice. He walked out of the room, lost in thought. These policemen were the first to push an honest, innocent common man towards crime and dishonest ways. Obviously, my brother was expected to go to 'any length' to arrange what they demanded. Within minutes, bhaiya was back and passed his phone to the policeman.

"Who is that?" The policeman sounded irritated.

"My dad," bhaiya replied.

The policeman and my father had a long discussion. I could not hear my father's words but it was clear that he was begging the policeman. He returned the phone to bhaiya. My brother moved out of the room.

"Do think about it again," my brother returned.

"How much can you arrange?"

"Sir! The mobile may hardly be of some 5000-6000 rupees."

"That is irrelevant. We are not here to assess the mobile's cost, but your brother and his friend's future. Your brother is charged with theft." He shook his head.

"I understand, sir. But consider our situation, we are just students."

"Give us five less. Fine?" the policeman said magnanimously.

"It's difficult to manage. The bank transaction hours are over."

"Borrow from your friends if you have to. Rich kids usually go to college," he said and smiled notoriously.

"It is a large sum."

The policeman took bhaiya out of the room. Another conversation. Finally, the policeman returned to the room, happy. He looked at both of us.

"You will be able to leave as soon as your brother returns. Your bad day will soon be over," he chirped.

He had come to an agreement with bhaiya. Gandhi ji hanging on the wall was still smiling. He seemed to have won again. The two of us had no choice. We couldn't stay in jail for two days, awaiting bail. The policeman stepped out as Sahil's uncle came to the police station.

"Don't worry. Your kid is safe here. We will let him out soon. We are just waiting for someone," he looked at the entrance. "And, there he is."

The policeman almost jumped with happiness as he saw bhaiya coming. Bhaiya handed something wrapped in an old paper to the policeman. "Count it."

"It's okay. We trust you. Plus, we know where you live," the policeman patted his shoulder.

Uncle, bhaiya and the policeman came back to the room.

"It's late. Leave now, you have to study for your exams," the policeman smiled sweetly.

I was surprised at the change in his behaviour. But bhaiya was not. A few pieces of paper with Gandhi ji's face on them were the reason behind the policeman's happiness. Their hard work of one week had paid off. The three personnel who had come to our flat in the morning came to drop us to Sahil's uncle's car.

"Don't do things like this again. Okay?" One said to me.

I didn't answer. The other extended his hand towards me, for a handshake, "Let me know if you have any problem next time."

We settled in Uncle's car. One of the policemen closed the car's door for me. Finally, uncle put the car into gear.

Suddenly my mind went back to the past. When I was a kid, my father used to tell me, "*Don't pick anything lying on the road.*"

Don't Booze

Did I sound toughened during my interaction with the policemen? That's because life had given me many lessons during my years of engineering. Some I have learnt, some not.

We were growing up fast in college. I met new people, new methods of enjoyment and its effects.

Coming back to the second semester again, the three of us sat on chairs opposite to the cash counter. We had discovered, there was a greater girl to boy ratio in medical colleges and College of Engineering for Women's canteens. Our canteen was always overcrowded with guys. The medical college canteen had beautiful girls from MBBS and BDS college. Most of them were very rich, high-maintenance, out of our league kind of girls. Girls from College of Engineering for Women were mostly from middle class families and were easier on our pockets. That was the reason Punit, Sahil and I spent most of our free time in that canteen.

"A Monday morning class with a hangover is rough man," Punit held his head.

"You had very little yesterday," Sahil refreshed Punit's memory.

"Yeah. Little." I made a face.

"C'mon dude! If we don't enjoy at this age, when will we?" Punit laughed, unpleasantly.

"I won't enjoy your way, ever."

"I too thought like you till sometime back. Once you get the taste, you can't stop yourself," Punit explained.

"Do we come here to convince one another to drink?" Sahil interrupted.

"Of course not," I replied.

"Then, order what you want to have."

"Dew for me," I said.

"Another for me," Sahil seconded.

"I will have a hot coffee. I need to keep my eyes open in class," Punit said in a lazy tone, stretching his stiff muscles.

Sahil went to the counter for coupons.

"So, plans for this semester?" I did not wish to suffer like the last.

"That girl looks nice," Punit commented about a girl behind us.

I turned to look at the girl. She was in a white and pink salwar-kameez. Her hair was open, most of it resting on the table. She held a cup of tea in one hand while with the other gripped a handkerchief and mobile, tightly.

"Isn't she pretty?" Punit was smiling like a fool.

"Yes, she is." I nodded.

"Let's ask her out."

"Are you in your senses? Why will a girl go out with anyone of us? Strangers! Aren't we?" I reasoned.

"C'mon man! We are men. Trying luck with every beautiful girl is our birthright," Punit dripped confidence.

Sahil came back carrying two Mountain Dew bottles and a cup of coffee.

"What do you think of that girl?" Punit pointed towards her.

"Only good thoughts," Sahil's eyes had turned into saucers.

"Mr Day Dreamer, have your coffee. Don't start staking claims on every girl you see here." I didn't like his idea to approach the girl.

"Look, the thing is…" he paused, checked to see if anyone could hear him, and spoke in a gentle tone again, "She does not seem to be from our college. Or, our dirty eyes would have caught her earlier. If she is from College of Engineering for Women, there is little chance that she knows any guy."

"What nonsense are you talking?" The alcohol had messed up my friend's head.

"Personal experience, man! We can all try our luck. What do you say?" Punit looked at both of us with excitement in his eyes.

"You are still not in your senses. How many pegs did you have yesterday?" Sahil shook his head, concerned for his friend.

"C'mon guys, I am fine. Let's do it, Viraj," he looked at me.

"You have lost it. I don't want my cheeks to be reddened."

"Look at her. Do you think she can harm a fly?" Punit looked at her delicate form.

"Whatever! I don't want to go back with red cheeks or an enriched vocabulary of abuses."

"Take it as a challenge. Whoever out of the three of us asks her out, will have to be treated by other two." Punit was hell bent on executing his plan.

"It's a deal," Sahil took the bait, ignoring me.

"Count me out. I have never been abused by a girl, and I don't intend to start now." I refused to play along.

"Another rule. If we or any of us is abused, other two will keep it a secret."

"Agree to that," I needed the protection deal.

Punit casually walked to the girl.

"I think we better get away, before a scene is created," I was only half kidding.

"Let's wait and watch. We will be out of here before they know we are with him," Sahil's words were malicious, but I knew it was only friend's love.

"Hi! I am Punit." I had never seen Punit smile quite in that way, lips slightly upturned. It did make him look cute.

"Ruhi." She had not taken offence, yet.

"I heard this evening is going to be life changing, what are you doing?" Punit's smile was only getting brighter.

"That depends on the options." She definitely seemed interested in the new guy with a cute smile.

"Well, *Rang De Basanti* released last week. Would that interest you?" He was all charm.

"Hmm... Time?"

"City Pride, Kothrud suits you?"

"At what time?"

"Let me get tickets first. Then, I will let you know," Punit said reasonably.

"Sure. I am running late for my classes," she started moving.

"Your number?" We thought he was pushing his luck. Even Ruhi looked surprised.

"How do you expect me to inform you about the timings of the show?" Punit was smooth.

They exchanged numbers. We didn't miss her lingering glance as she left the place. Punit walked towards us, his chest swollen to twice its original size.

"Why not take her to City Pride, Satara Road? I mean, it's close by, and will save time." My clever friend was not so clever, eh!

"Who wants to save time? The farther we go, more of gorgeous girl's company," he winked.

The reasoning was infallible.

$ON OF A RICH – Punit's tee declared. He and Ruhi had just come out of the theatre. Sahil and I were waiting outside for our friend.

"Interested in a round of drinks?" Punit asked.

"No, I am not," I declined.

"Ruhi and I are planning on going to a bar. It will be great fun," he said and turned to glance at Ruhi. She was waiting by a roadside stall.

We rode to Banjara Hills at Chandni Chowk. The road was treacherous and riding a bike was a pain. I had never been inside a bar before. The interiors had mellow bluish light. A soft, slow music filled the room. Punit and Ruhi sat together. Sahil and I sat opposite them.

"Whisky or vodka?" Punit asked her.

"Vodka," she grinned.

Punit ordered vodka for the lady, whisky for himself and the non-drinking partook of the roasted peanuts.

"One more, lady! One more, rock star!" Punit urged. The girl looked like she had hit her limit and gone beyond.

It was past eleven when we came out of the bar. Ruhi could not stand on her feet. Punit offered her his elbow, helping her walk to his bike.

"You follow us," Punit instructed.

I nodded. It took Ruhi three attempts before she could get on the bike. Before we could pick up speed though, she dropped her purse. The second time she did it, Sahil offered to carry it. We started our ride back to campus.

Punit rode very fast. We lost them in no time.

"I have to pee," Ruhi whispered into Punit's ears.

"Now?" Punit asked in astonishment.

"Yes, now."

On the right side of the road was a steep valley and on the left were the curving mountains. Small bushes lined the side of the road. Punit stopped his bike.

"Go."

"Where?" Ruhi looked around.

"There," Punit pointed to the bushes.

"No. I am scared," Ruhi screeched.

I noticed Punit standing on the road.

"Why are we stopping here?" I enquired.

"We will be back in two minutes," he left, holding Ruhi's hand.

They walked to the bushes. I was curious.

"Now hurry up," Punit whispered.

"It's so dark here," she giggled.

"Do you want me to come with you?" Punit offered.

"No, are you nuts! I am a girl," she declared.

"I think I have an empty Pepsi bottle in my bike. Can you manage in that?" Punit asked hesitatingly, not sure of the dynamics.

"Are you mad?" Ruhi asked incredulous.

"What do you want to do then?"

"Find a hotel, lodge, resort or anything, and fast. It's urgent."

"Hmm..." Punit was lost.

We found a resort on the Pune-Mumbai highway. Ruhi got down from the bike and waited while Punit came towards us.

"You guys make a move. I will see you in the morning," he sounded mischievous.

"Best of luck," Sahil raised his thumb, and handed Ruhi's bag to him.

Punit and Ruhi entered the resort together. The man at the reception was in his early thirties. He wore a monkey cap and a dirty yellow shirt. He grinned widely for his customers.

"Ch...Charge for a room?" Inexperience choked Punit.

"Three hundred for the night," the man smiled knowingly.

Punit searched for his wallet, when Ruhi caught his hand.

"Can we see the room before we decide?"

"Of course." The man took the set of keys from the hook. He unlocked a room and entered. Ruhi and Punit followed.

"What a fine room," the man exclaimed.

A double bed with clean white bed sheets stared at us. Two pillows occupied most of the bed. In a corner was a small television.

"Here is the washroom." The man opened another locked door.

Ruhi moved forward to have a close look. "Can I use it?"

"Yes please…"

She had dashed to the washroom before the man could answer her question, locking it from the inside.

"Lock the room from inside. I will make payment and come back," Punit yelled from outside. "Let's finish the formalities." He turned to the man.

Punit had just extended three hundred-rupee notes over the counter when someone caught his hand.

"The washroom is very dirty," Ruhi was very angry.

"I will get it cleaned early morning, ma'am."

"No," she refused. "Come darling, we will find a better place." She tugged Punit's tee and he followed her. The disappointed man watched their back as his three hundred rupees walked out the door.

"What were you paying him for? We did not actually need that room," Ruhi chuckled.

"I was not sure," Punit hid his emotions.

He kick-started his bike and drove towards the campus. She directed him to a friend's flat where she could stay the night, since entry to her hostel at that hour was impossible.

"Stop here," she pointed to a large building's gate.

Punit stopped his bike. She got down, waved at him and said, "Good night. Sweet dreams."

Punit waved back, without his cute smile. His dreams had been washed down the washroom's drain.

“One thousand seven hundred and ten,” Punit screamed the next morning as he checked the deductions from his card.

“What’s that?” Sahil asked struggling with his Graphics sheet.

“Cost of Punit’s attempt at happiness.” I was joyous. I was a true friend.

“What? You spent that much in a single day?” Sahil was surprised.

“Movies, popcorn, petrol, booze, bar, resort…claiming our birthright, that can’t be cheap,” I was having a great time out of my friend’s discomfort. “Trying our luck with every beautiful girl is our birthright,” I repeated Punit’s words.

Punit’s phone rang. He looked at the screen, puzzled.

“Hi! How are you?” the voice on the other end of the phone inquired.

“Never been better. What about you?”

“I am fine too. Did you sleep well last night?”

“Yes, yes…” he nodded.

“Can we go shopping today?” the voice asked.

“My bike’s tyre got punctured on the way to my flat last night.”

“Oh! Tough luck.”

“Indeed. Bye.” Punit disconnected the call.

“Who was that?” I asked eagerly.

“Ruhi,” he replied curtly.

“How did your bike get punctured?” Sahil asked, puzzled.

“It didn’t.” Punit sat on the chair under the fan.

“You two had fun yesterday, didn’t you? You enjoyed her company,” I was confused.

“Yes, I did. But, she is too costly,” he said and smiled cutely.

I had not tasted booze yet. My friend’s lesson did set an example. If only we could learn from others’ mistakes!

37 + Grace Marks

The rumours erupted every second day. *First year results are coming out today!* Two weeks were over, but there was still no sign of the awaited results. Students paid daily homage to the students' information section.

Finally, the day came. Nikhil and the others prayed and promised offerings at Ichha Poorti Temple in the back market, to Sai Baba in Shirdi, for a mark-sheet without 'Fail' inked on it. I had locked myself in my room – tensed, confused, out of breath. The moment we received the message, *'results out'* from a friend's number, Punit, Sahil and I sprinted out of our room.

College was different that day. Tensed faces, some unseen since semester's day one, had now appeared to crowd the balcony. One could get the actual count of the students in the first year that day. The students formed a queue and groups from the entrance of the north wing to the classrooms. Getting a foothold on the stairs was tough, because of the crowd. Some impatient souls went to the department enquiring, "Sir, when will the results be out?"

The staff ignored us. This was the day college staff lived for. Today they'd let everyone know their importance. Every peon thought of himself as the head of the institute. And then, in this chaos walked up a faculty member, and the GFM. The Guardian Faculty Member, who is responsible for reprimands on our poor performance in examinations, held bundles in both hands as if those were some dreaded weapons of mass destruction.

The GFM asked us to take our seats, three students on one bench. We listened to our faculties for the first time in our engineering life. This was their day!

The mark-sheets were distributed, one by one: Aakash, Abhishek and so forth. I could see a few faces glowing as soon as the mark-sheet reached their hands, while most underwent a ninety-degree downfall. All clear mark-sheets were a rarity. Back in a paper or two was common, and was distributed like sugary treats in a temple. The reaction was exactly opposite to a temple distribution. One who got least or none was more blessed. There were mark-sheets of all varieties, with two, four and some with even five backlogs.

I was cursing my parents for naming me Viraj. Fifteen minutes of the nerve-racking wait and Karan received his sheet! Karan pumped the air with joy and chuckled at his all clear mark-sheet.

Students left the room as soon as they had their fate in hand. Few including me were still waiting for fortune to make its decision. Thick bundles became thinner and thinner as my heartbeat turned slower and slower. Finally, a name boomed, "Viraj..."

I walked to the professor, took my mark-sheet and stepped out of the classroom. I closed my eyes and prayed to almighty before looking at the marks.

Subjects	**Total** (Out of 100)	
Engineering Mathematics-I	40	
Engineering Sciences-I	40	
Elements of Mechanical Engineering	31	F
Elements of Civil Engineering	40	
Elements of Information Technology	56	

It meant I had failed in one subject, got forty in three, which were the passing marks and had scored a 56 in IT.

Punit walked up to me. "Hey, how did you fare?"

I directed him towards the stairs silently.

"Come on man, stop that silent treatment. Do you have a backlog?" Punit tried to peek into my mark-sheet.

"Let's get out of here."

We moved downstairs. I handed my mark-sheet to him and took his in my hand.

"Just a single back! You should be happy."

"I managed to sail through three of them," I shivered to think, what if I hadn't?

"At least you cleared all other papers. Aakash could not clear any. Hemant has three backs." Punit boosted my morale.

"Yeah, that's the reason to celebrate. You got poor marks? So what? Compare it with the worst scorer of class and congratulate yourself," I said acidly. "What about Sahil's result?"

"Oh, I was so occupied with myself, I forgot all about him."

Punit called him up. He was at home, and yes with his mark-sheet. Three backlogs and the other two said forty.

I swore to myself that I'd work hard in the next semester and score better. These are the promises which every engineering student makes after poor results, but rarely keeps and ends up faring as badly in the semesters to follow.

Very few came to class the next day. The unfortunate bad scorers sat sadly in their rooms. The toppers were busy celebrating. A few toppers, the ones who had cleared all the papers, visited class, including Nimisha.

It's been a long while since I told you about her. I should, since she played such a crucial role at that juncture in my life. I remember things about her in their minutest detail. The shortest of conversations even.

The day after the results were declared, seeing her among the few present in class, I walked up to her. She stood with Vijay. I wanted to speak to her. I couldn't come up with the courage, so I turned to Vijay.

"How much did you score?"

"I got 67.5 %." Vijay adjusted his thick specs over his nose.

"That's great. You must be the class topper."

"No, Manan is topper of the class with 72 %," he said. "I am third," he added sadly.

Nimisha chirped, "He got one mark more than me." She attempted a sad smile, but I found it brilliant.

This was time for me to leave. Standing among class toppers, the question 'How much did you score?' would certainly crop up. I was not in a situation where I could reveal my marks to Nimisha. I was ashamed. I had fifteen percent less than her. I spotted Punit and strode towards him.

"Do you know something?" Punit asked as we were walking down the stairs.

"What?"

"Did you ask others about their results?"

"I know Manan is the topper of our class. Then Priyanshu, followed by Vijay and so on," I rattled.

"I didn't mean that. Did you see the marks scored?"

"No."

"Highest marks scored by any student who failed in a subject is 36."

"So what?"

"It means, if you scored 37, 38 or 39, the examiners stretched it to 40," Punit explained.

So, that was my story. I got 40 in three out of five subjects. I passed in three papers out of five, courtesy my teachers' grace. You've heard of first class and second class. Mine is not even a pass class. It is grace class, rather 37 + grace marks.

Cowardly to Meet

I bet, Valentine was not a saint, but a sinner. Because of him, a day was picked when every mooning idiot believes all his wishes will come true. One might not have the courage to speak about their feelings throughout the year, but come this day and heroism spreads like wildfire. The result is not always 'happily ever after' though. I was no different nor was my life. Nimisha entered my world months ago. So far I had not been able to exchange more than two words with her. I had chosen this day to change that.

"Have you considered your decision to call her?" Punit studied the ticking hands of the wall clock.

I turned to look at him inquisitively. He pointed at the clock.

"There are still five minutes left to midnight." I gazed at the clock.

You know what is the greatest invention for a heart in love? A telephone… a mobile… any communication device. It is a boon for lovers who are unable to open their hearts to the person it beats for.

We were on the road, searching for a coin-box telephone booth. Those were the days of red telephones, where one could drop a coin and talk to someone for sixty seconds. Every other shop had it.

Punit pointed at a shop in one corner.

"Yeah, let's go," I hastened to the red box.

The man inside me was shaking like a leaf. I believe, every guy is jarred to the bone before making a call to a beautiful girl, especially at midnight. I faced the coin box. Taking in a deep breath, I put in a coin, and dialled her number. My heart echoed the ringing tone's speed. The call was picked and my heart stopped.

"Can you give me two minutes of your time?" It was the weirdest opening line I had ever said.

"May I know who is this?" a surprised voice countered.

My mouth was glued for a few moments. I shook them open, "You don't know me by name," I lied.

"Still, I need to know if I am supposed to speak to you," she reasoned.

My mind went numb. I looked at the walls for inspiration. Surprisingly, there were no advertisements destroying the cleanliness of the walls, except a palmist's words written on the wall, '*Apna Bhavishya Janiye Know your Future. Call on 982344*****'.

"Bhav… Bhavishya." I stammered, while performing my second naming ceremony.

"Is that a real name?" she asked warily.

"What's wrong with the name?"

"It doesn't really sound like a name."

"Bhavishya Sharma." Life is about changes. Survival makes it necessary that with time we change whatever is required – Name, caste, community. Anything.

"Mr Sharma, why are you calling me at this hour of the night?"

"Were you busy?"

"Not really," she answered casually. "But how do you know me?"

"We are in the same college."

"From my class?"

"Yes, in your class."

"So, why don't you talk to me in class?"

"I cannot."

"Cannot?"

"Yes, I am not comfortable talking to girls, especially you," I explained.

"And, why is it so?" She giggled mischievously.

"Come on, don't laugh. You are special. I was driven to talk to you." That was the truth. Never before had any girl drawn me like Nimisha had.

"Who gave you my number?"

Damn! Why do girls ask so many questions?

"Men cross-over seven seas for a girl. Give me some credit, can't I find out a number on which my life depends?" I knew I sounded filmy, but at that moment, I couldn't care less.

"Oh please! Just tell me the name of the person who gave you my number?" Her tone had turned serious, as if she wanted to give the person a piece of her mind.

"Sorry. I promised the guy, his name will not be maligned for doing me the biggest favour. Don't ask me. His act means a lot to me."

"But why are you calling me?"

"Happy Valentine's day," I managed in my quivering voice. Weren't those words the purpose of this call?

"Thank you! Same to you," she replied easily.

"I was curious. Which lucky guy will be having the pleasure of your company today?" My heart thudded.

"No one."

"Really?"

"Yes. Can I go, Mr Sharma? It's late."

"With pleasure," I replied with a smile.

"Good night."

"Bye." I waited for her to disconnect.

Love lengthens days. It had been forty long hour since my ears last heard the sweetest voice in the universe. I did start with a lie, hiding my identity. To tell you the truth, courage does not come easy. There needs to be some encouragement, and so far, she had shown none. I planned to speak to her again. It was her birthday!

I banged the receiver down, after my third attempt went unanswered. The phone rang and rang on the other end but in vain. "*Where is she? Is she ignoring calls from unknown numbers? Did I say anything wrong that night? Did I offend her?*"

When you're in love, your heart keeps questioning your brain. Questions were rushing into my mind too. I reached Punit's place.

"She is not taking calls because she might be celebrating with her friends," Punit offered a possibility when he saw me in deep thought.

"Celebrations? All day? I have been calling her since morning. When will I wish her?" I was impatient. It didn't really make sense, but I had developed a tunnel vision where Nimisha was concerned. I had become too possessive.

"All you want to do is wish her, right? How about sending a message?"

"Not a bad idea. But if I do, she will know it's me." My mind was ticking.

"She can find out your number from our classmates, but not Sahil's," Punit suggested.

"You are right. Let me forward the message to his number." I began typing:

'Many happy returns of the day. Hope you get everything that brings smile to your face.:) Bhavishya.'

I was looking for Sahil's number, but my head was full of her.

"Oh shit shit shit!" I cursed. "I've sent it directly to her," I was appalled.

"Yay, party!" Punit cackled jumping from his place.

"Don't laugh, you jerk! It was a mistake. Oh, I better die in the next few minutes."

"It's done dude, you sent her a message. It's time to celebrate."

The thought of facing her the next morning in the class was intimidating. *Why did I have to prove myself a fool again? How do I escape? It will be no time before Diggy tells her that I was the one calling her.* Desperate, I sent the message again to Sahil's number and from there, forwarded it to Nimisha.

"What are you doing now? Sending it again and again?" Punit was surprised.

"If she asks me, I can say that message may have been sent by one of my friends. Sahil can save his own ass." I winked at Punit.

"Not bad, dude. Mischief of love, eh!" He grinned.

A girl's voice is sweeter than music when you're in love with her. I passed my days in the hope of hearing the music, thinking about her every moment. I had not been able to wish her on her birthday. I kept kicking myself about that. Her dazzling blue eyes did not allow me to sleep; my ears wanted to hear her and my mind always wanted to think about her.

Her number was on autodial in my mind. The fingers obeyed and her phone started ringing.

"Hello. Who is this?" The same sweet voice asked again.

"This is Bhavishya," I replied.

"Ah! Now you call," she sounded excited.

"I called on your birthday too. You didn't care to pick up the phone," I showed my disappointment.

"That day! I lost my mobile somewhere, so no one was able to speak to me. I apologize to you as well," she explained sweetly.

"In that case, belated happy birthday. Tell me how it was?"

"It was fun, thank you."

"What were you doing now?"

"Can I ask you something? Are you really from my class?" she changed the topic abruptly.

"Yes, I really am from your class," I emphasized.

"Why are you so afraid of me?" She was curious.

"I have not mastered the art of speaking to girls yet. You are the one who made me come out of my shell. No one else was worth it," I tried my best to explain.

"Why should I believe you are in my class?"

"I mark your proxy every time you are not there. Have you never wondered about your impeccable attendance score?" In college, there is no greater proof of love. I miss her when she is not there, but I make sure her fun time-out doesn't cost her.

"I have… now that you mention it. You do that? Aww… how sweet of you!"

I felt all my efforts had paid off. This was the lord granting me the sweetest blessings in Nimisha's voice.

"Yeah, I never miss doing it."

"Continue then. I am not coming tomorrow morning as well," she chuckled this time.

"Anything for you, ma'am."

"Hey, my friends are here. I have to leave. Can we talk some other time?" She was eager to end the conversation.

"Sure." Did I have a choice?

"Bye."

Long beeps trilled in my ear. She had disconnected the call, just like that. I couldn't let go of the phone for a while. I wanted to hear that tone that had filled me with unaccustomed happiness. There was so much more to say. The days got longer. The night went sleepless.

Music was more melodious, the grass got greener, the sky turned bluer. I felt her presence around, stronger, every moment.

"I have missed you," I said as soon as she picked up her phone.

"Who is this?" she asked.

"This is Bhavishya." I have found this was the big trouble with a coin box. Every time I called her, I had to introduce myself, anew.

"It's time you told me your real name," her voice turned serious in no time.

"I told you Bhav… Bhavishya Sharma." How a mere change in her tone was able to shake me up.

"Don't lie to me. Have the courage to be true about your name at least. Liar!" Her rude tongue was let loose on me.

"How can you be so sure?" I challenged.

"There's no one named Bhavishya Sharma in my class. You are not the only one who has access to the attendance sheet." I knew she was clever, but the proof of her intelligence was harming me.

"Are you sure? I may have been absent the day you checked the attendance sheet."

"Don't lie to me now. I am dead sure."

I was going to be dead soon, for sure. I had no option but to confess.

"This is not Bhavishya." The words left my mouth and sweat oozed from every pore of my body. What was it about girls and their commands?

"Tell me something I don't know. Who are you?"

"I can't tell you. I am really sorry." I knew I was being extremely stupid, but did I have a choice?

"And, why is that?"

"You know… I am afraid of you," I said pitifully.

"Still…" She must have grinned for the first time since I called that day.

"Yes."

"Come and meet me in class tomorrow. Only then we can chat on the phone."

"You are asking for the impossible," I was shaking again.

"Then these phone conversations are impossible."

Was she still laughing at my helplessness?

"Give me some time. I promise I will meet you soon."

"Time granted, Mr Sharma," she giggled. I knew she was not merciless.

"You are extremely kind, Ms Rungta." This time I could smile. "By the way, is your father into Apiculture? Honey making?" I asked casually.

"No. What made you ask that?"

"I was wondering, what has made you so sweet?"

"Very funny… It doesn't really feel like this is your first attempt at talking to girls."

"What does your father do?" I asked seriously.

"He works at AIIMS. He is a surgeon there."

"What about your mother?"

"She is a doctor too."

Only two doctors, blessed souls, could create someone so lovely.

"What are you thinking?"

I was silently lost in my thoughts. "Hey, are you there?" she asked again.

"Nothing. May I take your leave now?" I asked her permission.

"You may, Mr Sharma."

I disconnected the phone, with her thoughts in my head. A smile on my lips, I walked towards Punit's flat.

It had almost been a month since we had commenced our phone conversations. I never thought a girl could talk to me without knowing who I was. Books, studies, friends – I no longer cared about these things. Nimisha's pleasant voice, sweet talks, her laughter, her scolding, the little time that we had together, when we existed only for each other, no one came between us, no one mattered. She was all I needed to make me happy. However, there is a world outside, a world that does not always give what you want from it.

The tallest guy from IT Department, Sahil's friend, was a frequent visitor to Sahil's place – Shashank aka Sash to his friends. I had met him a couple of times. He was about to leave when I reached there.

"Hi Viraj. How are you?" Sash looked at me.

"I am fine. What about you?"

"I am good. Was just about to leave. Let's meet up soon." He shook hands and walked out of the door.

Punit smiled at me silently. I gave him a queer look. He wanted to tell me something, and what I heard was a blow that I felt in every cell of my body.

"Sash proposed to Nimisha," Punit said blankly.

The words made the floor slip from under my feet. I was a fool, believing us to be in love. I knew I loved her. I also knew she did not love me in the same way. But I had thought I had carved my spot in her life. I was hurting when I looked at Punit.

"It's not a joking matter. Stay out of it."

"I am not kidding," he said. "If you don't trust me, ask Sahil. Didn't he say that?" He turned towards Sahil.

Sahil looked at me meaningfully.

"What bullshit? How can he do that? He knows I like her." I was getting angry.

"How is anyone to imagine that you like her? She has been in college for more than a semester now. You may have been talking to her for a month, but did you even tell her your name? How can she like a guy whom she doesn't even know?"

"What did she tell Shashank?" was all I could think about.

"Nothing concrete. It was not a yes from her end, but how long do you think a girl like Nimisha will stay single?"

"What should I do?"

"You need to meet her. She should know whom she has been talking to," Punit advised.

I thought for a few minutes. Punit made sense. If it was not for friends who pushed forward, most of the love stories in this world would remain incomplete. *I should meet her once. She needed to know about the guy who was talking to her.*

"Let's go."

Sahil, Punit and I ran out of the room. Not to meet her, but to a place that connected us – a coin box telephone booth. I put a coin in the box and dialed her number. The phone started ringing.

"Hi. It's Bhavishya," I said.

"Tell me."

"You want to meet me, right?" I asked.

"Of course," Nimisha said.

"Tomorrow?" I checked.

She paused and then asked, "Are you no longer scared of me?"

"I am, but the need to meet you is stronger than my fear."

"Fine. We will talk during break," she said.

"Not in class. Can we meet at some other place? I mean outside college."

"I don't have conveyance. How will I return?"

"I will drop you back to your place on a bike."

"It's like... I don't sit with anyone on every other bike, Mr Sharma," she said and laughed.

"I will arrange for a bike on which you've already sat, Ms Rungta."

"Thanks a lot, Mr Sharma. I would prefer to walk."

"As you please. Let's meet at the ice cream parlour," I suggested.

"All those places are too far for me."

"When I say I will drop you, that's a problem. You have a problem in walking too. Why don't you buy a car, Ms Rungta?"

"That's a different topic. Classroom is the most suitable place."

"I would prefer living a few more days. Not in a hurry to die."

"Who is going to kill you?"

"Let it go. Tell me a place other than our class and the back market. I will come there."

"Fine," she said and continued after a moment's thought, "We will meet at 5.30 p.m. after classes are over. Outside the library?" she suggested.

"There will be lots of people around at 5.30."

"Oh my god! I don't want to meet you. The most cowardly creature of the world."

"Cool down, I will be there at 5.30," I gave in. I had to prove that I was not a coward.

Punit and Sahil were smiling at me.

"What makes you so happy?"

"She calls every guy there," Punit gurgled.

"She called Shashank to the same place," Sahil said.

Punit and Sahil were laughing. I was tense thinking about my situation. What was going to happen the next day?

Jazzy Love

It was a warm, sunny morning. I rushed towards college to attend my first lecture. It was a special day. Our college had been trying many new trends. Among those was a day for formals, when we were not allowed to wear casuals. I saw her. She was wearing a beautiful green salwar-kameez.

Who wanted to sit in class and stare at boring equations, when everyone had gone through so much trouble to look good? By half past two, no one was in the mood to suffer anymore. We decided to mass bunk and the gates were closed with everyone out of it.

About an hour before I was scheduled to meet her, I dialled her number.

"Where are you?" I asked as soon as she picked up my call.

"At my friend's place," she replied.

"Don't tell me that you are not coming."

"Don't worry," she chuckled. "I will be there."

I disconnected the phone, looked at Punit and smiled, "She is coming."

"Congrats man. Be ready for your first date."

It is really confusing what to wear when meeting a lovely girl. I had nearly emptied my cupboard. The best of my clothes didn't look good enough.

"Wear anything. Why are you so confused? She has seen you in your worst. You are in the same class, remember?" Punit mocked.

I finally decided on a white shirt and a pair of blue jeans. Punit and I were crossing the library within five minutes on Punit's bike.

"Let's wait at a distance from the place." We were at the parking.

We sat on a wall near the bike stand. Twenty minutes later, she hadn't come.

"Let me give her a call."

"You are going to look for a coin box now?"

"That ends today," I said pulling out my mobile.

I called her number. She picked the call on the first ring.

"Come to the library," she responded even before I could introduce myself.

"See you," I disconnected.

"Punit, wait here. I will be back soon."

Punit raised his thumb.

When I reached the library, she was there, waiting. She was wearing the same green salwar-kameez that she had worn in the morning. I haven't seen an angel, but I could bet she looked far more exotic than one. She smiled at me. I was sure she was a magician. Who else knows the art to thump hearts just by a single glance? A fragrance spread in the environment as she clutched her dupatta with her left hand. We shook hands. Her palm was cold to touch.

"I knew it was you."

"Really?" I asked her.

"Yes. Though we haven't talked much in class, I could recognize your voice."

She continued telling me how she knew it was me. I didn't care what she said then. For me, it was the day of my life.

"Don't call me anymore," she said.

"What if I feel like talking to you?"

"We are classmates. We can always chat in class."

"Hmm…" I nodded.

"I have to go now."

"*So early,*" I wanted to say. "Do you have some work?" I ended up asking instead.

"Yes, Akriti is waiting for me at the podium."

I didn't want her to go. She had just come, and she wished to leave. "Can't you stay a while?"

"There is nothing much to say. I would rather spend some time with my friend."

I looked at her. She really wanted to leave and I really wanted her not to.

"Bye." She turned to leave.

"*Almighty, what should I do to stop her?*" I asked God. "I think, I love you!" I almost shouted.

She turned, "Please... don't use the word 'love.' How can one go about exploiting that word? Everyday someone or the other falls in love. Is it that easy? I am tired of hearing it again and again!" Her outburst matched my emotions.

Silence followed. She was right. A girl would get irritated if after every two to three days, a new guy would come and say that he had feelings for her. I had made the same mistake. I hadn't planned on saying it to her so early. It wasn't supposed to be like this. What had come over me?

"I am leaving now. Bye." She raised her two fingers to wave at me.

I waved my hand to bid her goodbye. I reached the parking. Punit wasn't there. I called him, "I told her."

"What did you tell her?"

"What can I tell a girl whom I have been calling continuously?"

"What did she say?" Punit was as astonished at my action as I was.

"She was frustrated with so many proposals in her life." An unwilling smile appeared on my face.

"It's okay man. Very few girls say 'yes' on the first day. All guys are not as handsome as me," he said and smiled.

"Fine, Mr handsome. Let's go. Where are you?"

"On my way."

Two days later, it was Holi. I thought of wishing her on the phone and dialled her number.

"Who is it?"

"I think you can save my number now."

"I will surely do that." She recognized my voice. "So, why did you call me?"

"Happy Holi, Ms Rungta."

"Same to you, Mr Aron."

"Thank you."

"You are most welcome. Can I go now?"

"Are you busy with something?"

"Yes, sort of."

"But, you didn't give me an answer." Punit had said, a girl never replies positively in the first go. I thought I would push my luck again. Maybe the days in between had made her reconsider.

"Look!" Her voice became stern. "Viraj, you are not going to gain anything."

"Who said that I did it to gain anything? A few things in life are beyond profit and loss." And, love was surely one of them. I smiled at those words.

"I don't want a long discussion about this. Can I hang up?"

"As you wish. Happy Holi again."

"Thanks," she said and disconnected the phone.

I have always seen it happening with a guy. When you are a good friend, you are a hero. But when you want to become more than a friend, you become a villain. Girls and their attitudes are quite difficult to understand. I called her a few more times in the days that came. She always tried to ignore me. The duration of the calls decreased with time. News about love travels with the speed of light. A lot of her friends and a few of mine came to know about us. Some shushed conversations were heard. I tried to see things her way. Maybe it was hurting her image. I decided to give my impulses a rest.

📖

With time, I started caring about other things in life. I started meeting friends and friends started their games. I was at Praneet's place that day.

"Do you know something?" Praneet asked me.

"About?"

"About Nimisha… She is not a nice girl."

"C'mon dude. Don't say anything you feel like." My mood was ruined as soon as I heard the first negative thing about her.

"It's not something I feel. You know very little about her." He shook his head in pity.

"I am happy knowing as much I do."

"Do you know that she has a boyfriend?" he said, looking straight into my eyes.

"No, she doesn't." My heart-rate had begun to slow down.

"Every evening after class, a Karizma waits by her hostel and she goes out on it," Praneet continued ignoring my mood.

"Don't lie."

"Look. I just want you to know the truth."

"I am happy knowing the unreal her."

He tried to console me with small talk. But when you are actually sad, nothing can give you comfort. So far I had made peace with what happened between us. But this conversation had brought back everything I had been trying to leave behind. I left Praneet's hostel thinking about Nimisha.

I wasn't too sure about Praneet's story about Nimisha. *But, what would he get by lying to me?* There were questions running in my mind. I wanted to say to my heart, "*Everything is fine.*" It replied, "*Do you really think everything is fine?*" I somewhere knew it was not.

How can she do that? Our conversations had meant something. How could we have lasted as long as we did, otherwise? I did lie about my name but was honest about everything else. I told her the feelings I have for her. She was with someone else? How could she do this to me? I didn't have an answer. When you love someone deeply, possessiveness comes as a free gift.

What happened next was unplanned. But I had no idea how to stop it. Was I proud of doing it? I have looked back on the incident a number of times, and every time I come up with the same answer. I was absolutely wrong. I wish I had realized it earlier.

We had finished dinner. Punit knew that I was disturbed. He came to my place with Sahil.

"I really need to clarify it. I can't let it go as if nothing has happened. How can she do this to me?" I asked Punit.

"A few days back, you were proclaiming your love for her. Now, you can't trust her?" Punit thought I was overreacting. "The best gift you can give to your loved ones is your trust."

"I did that. I need to know what is going on in her mind. She can't just continue to ignore me. I must mean something to her."

"Give her a call if you want to. Maintain your cool," he advised.

Punit and I went to the terrace of my flat. Involuntarily, I dialled her number.

"I needed to talk to you," I said abruptly.

"I am busy right now."

"I have to talk, now."

"Sorry." She disconnected the phone.

"She doesn't even want to talk to me anymore! There were days when she talked without knowing who was at the other end," I said annoyed.

"C'mon Viraj. She might be busy. It's not like she won't ever talk to you." Punit tried his best to comfort me.

The phone started vibrating. "Who the hell is this?" I shouted. Before I could pick the call, it was disconnected. A missed call on my phone. It was her number.

"It was Nimisha, right? I told you. She does care about you. That's the reason she gave a missed call. Call her now and talk to her," Punit encouraged like a true friend.

I dialled her number.

"You were about to say something?" she said directly.

"Where are you right now?" My tone was doubtful.

"How does that concern you?" she challenged.

"It does not have anything to do with me, right?" She was not helping my mood.

"No. It should not matter to you."

There is just a single letter's difference between anger and danger. And once you are governed by the first one, the latter follows.

"You know? You were right to stay away from me. You don't deserve to be cared for, to be my girlfriend. You lack character, you are just a…"

"Sorry, I didn't hear you. Could you please repeat yourself?" she interrupted.

My words were shaking but the anger was not. "Ms Rungta, I am extremely sorry to say these words. But I feel that you don't have the character to be my girl." I had no words left.

However, there was something going on at her end. I didn't know about it then. She was at the volleyball ground with her friends, practicing volleyball for the college team. Most of them were boys from my class. They had asked her about the person on the other end of the phone when she disconnected my call for the first time. They forced her to give me a missed call. And, when she had asked me to repeat myself, she had put the phone on loudspeaker.

"How dare you say that!" A male voice exclaimed.

I was shocked, "Who is there?"

"Tera baap," the voice roared.

"Hey! Is that you, Ankur?" I recognized the voice.

"You son of a bitch. How dare you say those words to a girl?" Another voice shouted.

"Vikram?" I was confused. My classmates, all in one place! I couldn't really make out who was on the other end of the phone. They were all shouting, abusing. Nothing was heard clearly. I felt like I was underwater, unable to breathe. Something very wrong had happened and I knew it was my mistake.

"It's not important who is on this line. It's important what you are saying to a girl, and that too your a classmate. You are way... way... out of line. How dare you?" A loud voice asked.

"Can you all let me explain...?"

"No, we won't. Don't you ever call her again!"

Who were these guys to order me! I was as much her classmate as they were! "Who wants to call her? Just hand her the phone for the last time. I need to end everything."

Punit understood from my reaction that something was going wrong. He stood beside me, trying to hear what was being said.

"You still have the guts to ask to speak to her? If we find you anywhere near her, disturbing her after this, you are dead. You hear? You will be dead..." somebody growled.

"Fuck off. Give her the mobile!" I shouted at the top of my voice.

"No," somebody said and disconnected the phone. I had not been able to speak to her. The last exchange was booming in my ears.

"Who was the guy?" Punit asked me.

"I don't know. The phone was rotating between Ankur, Vikram, Diggy and... I don't know." I sounded as confused, angry, frustrated as I was feeling inside.

"These bastards, they think you are alone. They can't say anything and just get away," Punit was not going to let me lose the battle. He took out his phone and dialled some numbers.

"What do you think? Viraj is alone. If you think that, you are making a big mistake."

"What are you saying, Punit? What happened?" The voice on the other end of the phone asked.

"What happened? You abuse a guy, threaten him. Do you think he is alone?"

"I am not getting you. What are you saying?"

"Where are you right now?"

"At Richie Rich."

"What is she doing there?"

"Who?"

"Are you with Nimisha and all?"

"No, I am not. What happened? Will you tell me?" the confused voice asked.

"Ankur, Vikram and others were abusing Viraj."

"Can you come and meet me now?"

"Sure. Call all the bastards there. They must know everything loud and clear."

The phone was disconnected.

He was talking to Ritesh, a common friend of Punit and Nimisha. He was the guy who had given Punit her number when I had needed it. We came down from the terrace to our rooms.

"Come with me. We are going to Richie Rich right now," Punit ordered me. "Sahil, go and call Lamboo from his room. We might need him."

Friends are like that. If you are sizzling inside, their blood boils too.

"Let it go man. I don't want this to go on and on. Me telling her something, they telling me off, you ruining your relation with everyone. It's not right. It needs to end." I sat on the chair opposite the bed.

"It's already on the verge of breaking. Get ready now." He pushed me to move my bum.

We hurried towards Richie Rich. Sahil went to Lamboo's place. Lamboo was a kind of a 'bhai' in college who was involved in fights at different levels.

Ritesh was waiting for us at Richie Rich. "What happened?" He extended his hands to shake.

Punit recounted the incident.

"But Viraj should not have said that," he said finally.

"She should not treat him the way she does," Punit replied. True friends stand by you even after seeing your most negative side.

"Anyway…"

"Did you ask them to come?" Punit asked.

"Yes, I spoke to Ankur. He will be here with Vikram and Diggy soon."

We could hear their bikes even from the distance.

"Be calm Viraj," Ritesh said to me, moving his hand downwards to ask me to lie low.

"I am. Don't worry."

The three of them barged towards me and Punit. Punit was ready for the fight. I was not.

"Punit. Just wait here for a while," I pushed him back so that I could talk to them on my own.

"But…"

"Please. I started this, let me finish it," I requested him.

He was livid. The look in his eyes was menacing. I didn't say anything.

I was standing with three other classmates of mine who had surrounded me from all sides. I stood with my legs apart, hands intertwined behind my back. I looked them in the eyes and said, "It could have been sorted once and for all if you would have only bothered to ask her to come along. If I could sort it out with her, that would have been the end of the matter. But, I guess, you want to deal with this matter by hitting me. Go ahead, hit as hard as you can."

I don't know why I said those last words. Punit stood at a distance. He could not hear me. Even I was not aware what was in store for me in the next minutes.

"Are you mad? We don't want to fight," Vikram said as he stepped towards me.

"If you think I am wrong, then…" I was cut short.

"We have to study together for the coming four years. How can we hurt each other?" Vikram said.

"But you know, the way you spoke to her was not right," Ankur admonished.

"I am tensed buddy. I heard something... My only truth is that I love her."

"There is nothing called love. At this age, we just have a little attraction towards a girl. That's it," Ankur averred.

"You shouldn't call a girl if she doesn't want to talk to you," Diggy joined him.

"I called her for the last time."

"Still, your attitude was not at all fair," Ankur repeated.

"You won't call her anymore, we hope?" Vikram asked, keeping his hand on my shoulder.

"No, I won't," I said, startled by Vikram's behaviour.

"End of discussion then. There is no space for differences among friends," he moved towards his bike.

Vikram waved as he left. Diggy left a smile and Ankur just moved away. I jogged to Punit.

"So… what was the outcome?" Punit asked.

"It's over. I am not going to call her anymore."

Punit nodded.

"Let's do the dew," I said as I saw Sahil coming.

We ordered three bottles of Mountain Dew for each of us while Lamboo ordered tea for himself. He smiled when he saw me. I smiled back.

We entered our compound with the bottles in our hands. I returned to my room after another half an hour. Punit and Sahil went to theirs. I thought a lot about what I had done that day. I knew it had been my mistake. Not hers. Also, true love is when you don't care whose mistake it is, but take the first step to save your relation. With a lot of guilt, I fell asleep that night.

No volume of guilt can change the past. You have to carry it with you in your heart, in your mind like that part of your body which doesn't function, which doesn't do any good to you. Worrying about it increases your burden. I went to college with a heavy heart the next day.

Nimisha sat in the adjacent row. Her face was expressionless. I looked at her for two entire lectures. I wanted to apologize for my harsh words the previous night. I wanted to apologize for having behaved like a guy that I wasn't.

As soon as the bell for lunch rang, I put my notebook and pen in my rucksack and moved towards the door, waiting for her to leave the classroom. She chose to walk out with Diggy. I followed her downstairs, looking for an opportunity to speak, but failed since some other classmates joined her.

Disappointed, I walked towards the library to return a book that I had borrowed a few weeks back. Some ten minutes later, when I came out of the library, I found Nimisha standing alone.

"What I did, is already done. I can't change it. I stand here in front of you, guilty. You can punish me," I said finally, lowering my eyes.

"Forget everything," she said. She was ready to leave.

Maybe she was right. I should forget everything after what I did.

"I promise I will. Just help me a little here." My eyes were a picture of sorrow. She waited for me to finish.

"Can we walk?" I am not sure when both my hands had clasped together. She looked at them.

"Look Viraj…" I knew she would say no if I let her finish.

"Please, don't say no. This is the only time I will ask you. Never again. Trust me." I don't know if she saw the tears in my eyes but the choking voice couldn't be missed.

"Okay."

We took the road towards the College of Engineering for Women. The sky was fast losing its color. Like I knew these were my final moments with Nimisha. After this, the sky and I will have to live in eternal darkness. Well, the sky had hope of a sunrise tomorrow. I was not going to have any such luck.

"Nimisha, you are friendly with everyone, boy or girl," I was not looking at her, I could not. "You were always so sweet with me…

well, before we met. What changed Nimisha? Did you find me so revolting?"

"It has nothing to do with you, Viraj." Her voice was gentle. "I have a problem with the mindset that a girl has to attach herself to some boy. A single girl cannot exist. I want to stay single, just because I enjoy it."

I nodded.

"Why should I give in to anyone because they think they can have a claim on me, simply because no one else has? I am my own person. I want to stay like that. I am more than a pretty girl. I am an individual who wants to live her life freely. Without the burden of someone else's feelings. I don't want that responsibility. I hope you understand now. It's not about me liking or disliking you. It's about me loving myself. I don't want anyone else to do that for me." Her voice had a seriousness I had never felt before.

The roads went silent. There was nothing in the world that could follow what that unique girl had expressed.

"Can we stay friends?" I still couldn't let go.

"I believe too much has happened to make it possible. It's all water under the bridge now, but I would prefer if we stick to our circles of friends," she finished.

She was right. I left her near the entrance of her hostel. It was not what I wanted. To let her go. But at least now I had some answers. I felt as if a weight had lifted off my shoulder.

I decided to concentrate on my studies.

There were two months left for the exams. I had to study well as I wanted to score good marks. Time passed and I made myself believe that I had no feelings for her. The semester exams were over. I could attempt most of the questions this time. In the month of July, we were promoted to the second year of engineering.

Survival of the Fittest

We read the term 'survival of the fittest' in standard eight in our Biology books, but understood the importance of this term on the day of our first year results. Every alternate boy or girl who received their mark-sheet had lost a year in college. College had a simple policy. If one wished to enjoy a little in college by ignoring studies, college gave a full year to enjoy life. The rule in college was to carry a maximum of three backs to the next year, that too with the result mentioning 'FAIL ATKT' (Allowed to Keep Term) on the mark-sheets. More than three backlogs meant a year's holiday to prepare for your papers.

Drops from Misha's eyes were wetting Niyati's tee as she held her in her arms, a mark-sheet with four backlogs fluttering in her hands. She could not even cry for her own marks. She had managed to clear the year. What if she had three backlogs? Everyone was disappointed that day. If not for themselves, then for his or her friends.

Punit and I walked out of the classroom after collecting our mark-sheets, cursing the examiner for checking our papers with extra devotion. I got three backs in my mark-sheet that semester. I had a companion with exactly the same number of backlogs, and it was none other than Punit. We were riding towards his flat.

"We studied more than last time and look! Three backlogs! Can you believe that? What a mess." I checked my mark-sheet for the tenth time, as if reading it again and again would increase my marks.

"I can't believe it's my result. It feels like they have given someone else's mark-sheet to me." Punit parked his bike and we climbed the stairs.

"From one to three. What progress in a single semester!"

Punit threw his rucksack on the bed, then followed it with his body.

"These examiners bring marks from their home. If they give all of them to us, what will they be left with?" I was in a rotten mood.

"Playing with our careers! Are they allowed to do that?"

"If we get marks like these, what kind of future will we have?" I was tensed.

"Companies here visit for 55%. Anyone will recruit us in the end."

"Is getting a small job from campus the only thing we want? We worked hard to get here. We deserve better marks. At least better than what we have here." I threw my mark-sheet on the bed.

"We have to work hard to get better marks," Punit observed philosophically.

"What if we want to go out for an off-campus?"

"You think too much," Punit declared.

"If I want to sit for Google, why will they shortlist my resume? Answer me."

"They won't. You know that."

"What's the use of doing this engineering then? If Google is my dream, and I know that is never going to get fulfilled." I was very upset. My future, my parents' expectations – everything was on the line.

"Look, our university gives, say 70% to a topper, another university gives 90%. You can't say they are better qualified for a job at Google."

"What about the recruitment process? If you own a company, who would you like to shortlist for an interview?"

"Definitely a 90% holder."

"Do you think that a 90% holder knows any more than the topper here?" I looked around for the mark-sheet I had thrown.

"I am not sure. We have good methods of practical and orals here. Other engineering colleges don't even have those."

"Then, why are they better than us?"

"There are loopholes in the education system," Punit philosophized, again.

"Our toppers here have 70%, in Orissa they get 90%. In Tamil Nadu engineering colleges as well. And 80% in colleges of Karnataka. I don't understand, why are marks the only criteria for shortlisting candidates?"

"That's how it is." Punit shrugged.

"We are failures then."

"There may be a few companies who do not recruit marks, but talent. Marks matter for just a few years after we pass out. The rest depends on our talent, how we use it to shape our life."

"Do you think it's the correct method to judge students? Hopeful freshers. How discouraging!" Failure sat heavily on my shoulders.

"No, that is definitely not. Do think about the IITs and NITs. They go for a CGPI system, where you don't have marks."

"How do they do it?"

"They take marks scored by you, divide it by marks scored by the topper and multiply it by ten. They get an equivalent score in ten."

"But, that will give someone a CGPI of ten."

"Few get that."

"How do companies recruit then?"

"As far as I know, they consider an 8.4 pointer as 84%."

"Oops. So again, everyone is ahead of us."

Punit did not reply.

"There should be some revolution in the education system. We can't compare guys from IITs and NITs with other engineering colleges. Moreover, there are no true scales to compare marks of students from different states. Similar is the case with state boards."

"That will take many long years."

"Hmm…"

We remained thoughtful after the rant.

Punit's elder brother came to visit him. He scolded Punit. Sahil and I were of no help at that moment. Sahil was disheartened. He could not clear a single paper that semester, and was listed to enjoy for the year.

The next day, Punit and I went to class. The room looked quite different that day. Most of the seats were vacant. We found out that seventy out of one hundred and thirty-five students would not be studying with us for the next year.

"*How can we study like this? We have an empty class.*" I asked myself.

But the college had already made arrangements. We saw many new faces in the second year class. There were a lot of students who were given a year to enjoy the previous year. After their enjoyment, they were attending classes with us. However, they were not enough. There were other ways to fill up the class. The college took a few students in each section through lateral entry. These were the students who did diplomas. If the classroom still looked empty, the college had another solution. They took out forms for the change of branch for any student from a lower discipline, who had scored good marks, and had dreamt of studying computer engineering. All was set for the department.

I went to class alone those days as Punit rarely liked coming to class after his bad results. I sat on the last bench of the second row, alone. I felt unhappy without my friend. So I decided to shift to the first bench of the second row, where another boy sat alone.

"Hi. Is anybody sitting here?" I enquired.

"No."

"Can I?"

"Yes, sure."

The Maths professor came in a few minutes. She wrote a question on the board and the guy on my right came up with the answer almost instantly. The same continued for the next three to four questions. My mind went in deep thoughts. *Who was beside me? Hope he is not the university topper.* There was news around that the university topper had joined the computer engineering course. We had no idea who he was. Another interesting story that we had heard about the university topper was that he had got 74% aggregate, but he got a back in Engineering Graphics. He got 26 out of 100 in that subject. However, based on his performance in other subjects, he was given a jack of 14 marks to pass in the subject, making him the university topper for this year.

I stared at his face after the classes were over. He was a dark chap. If the people who developed English similes saw him, they would change the simile '*as black as coal*' to '*as black as Muthu*'. Muthu Ramaswamy was his name. A dry tilak in combinations of red, orange and yellow ran between his eyes to his forehead. He used coconut oil or some equally bad smelling oil instead of hair gel to set his hair in place. He was not the university topper. He had scored a percent less than the topper and had changed his branch from Production Department. He came from a large family of engineers and all his cousins knowingly or unknowingly were computer engineers. How could he be different from them? He was just a follower.

Second Chance

A square cake covered in billowy whipped cream, a circle of red cherries and dark chocolate shavings was kept in front of me. After living together for over a year, Punit and Sahil knew a lot about my likes and dislikes, just as I knew about them. They had chosen this special Black Forest cake and were at my place in the middle of the night. Why? Because it was my birthday. Sahil put five candles on top of the cake and lit it. A couple of minutes had passed after midnight; the cake had been cut, a part was eaten and most of it was drying on our faces. A large portion was being enjoyed by the floor as well.

My phone rang several times during the cake cutting process. Few of the calls were answered, some went unanswered.

It was around 12:30 a.m. when Diggy's number flashed on my mobile. We were done cleaning our faces and preparing to leave for Richie Rich to celebrate the occasion. Sahil checked his face for remains of the cake in the mirror.

"Happy birthday, dude! Wish you a great year ahead," Diggy said, as soon as I picked up his call.

"Thank you," I replied with a smile on my face.

"So, what's the plan for the big day?"

"Nothing much. Going to Richie Rich right now. Want to join us?" I offered.

"Too late, man. Just changed and got into bed," he declined.

"Okay. Not an issue."

"What else?"

When you are deeply in love with someone, they are always the first in your thoughts. You always look for opportunities to get close to them. My love for Nimisha wasn't any exception. It was this question of Diggy's which triggered my mind to make plans for the day.

"I need a small favour from you. I want to celebrate this special day with Nimisha."

Diggy turned silent, taken by surprise.

Finally, he said gravely, "You know she doesn't like you much. Why don't you allow her to stay in peace?"

"I wish it could have been as easy."

"You promised us that you wouldn't interfere in her personal life, didn't you?" Diggy reminded me of my promise.

"Maybe I have presented myself in the wrong light where Nimisha is concerned. You've known me for over a year now. Do I seem like a person who would harm others?" I questioned.

"Viraj! Man, that's not the issue…"

"Certain events have occurred in such a way that she doesn't like me much. I am unable to change what has already happened, but I want to correct the wrong. I don't want her to keep any ill-feelings in her heart. I might have failed as a friend to you all as well, but I am burdened with this knowledge. Will you not help me come out of it? I want to throw a party and take all of you out. Please join me on this big day in my life." I managed to say all that had been troubling me for days.

Punit looked at me in awe as he heard me.

"Sorry Viraj. It won't be possible. Also, we are going..." Diggy stopped himself.

"You all are going to…?" I asked.

"Forget it. You enjoy your special day."

"You want me to enjoy it, right? Every year on their birthday, one should get a chance to start anew. Can't you give me another chance?"

The phone went silent. I could feel the ticking in Diggy's head. "We all are going out. It won't be possible, Viraj."

"I'm not asking you to cancel your plans. Why don't you allow me to be the host?" I insisted as if my life depended on it.

"If you really want to spend the day with her, you can come to Dev Uncle's Kitchen, Kondwa, tomorrow around 8 p.m. But don't be…"

His concern was cut short, "Don't worry. I will take care. Thank you!" I smiled.

"Happy birthday again. Good night," Diggy said and disconnected the phone.

What is it about the hope of meeting your beloved that enlivens your heart, sparks your mind, and spreads joy on your lips?

Punit understood my happiness. He hit me hard on my back, almost shouting, "I believe, this wouldn't hurt you anymore."

Vikram, Nimisha, Diggy, Riya, Ankur, and Ritesh were all settled around a heptagon wooden table. A few half-eaten dishes in front of them showed they had been there for some time. I wished we had reached a little early.

Mud walls with several animal crafts and *ektara* placed on it gave the place a village like feel. The old wooden door only accentuated the effect. A pitcher with a long neck and lanterns on the rack above the door added to the looks. A not-so-bright light on the ceiling contributed to the ambience.

I asked Punit to sit at the table opposite to the group and made my way to the washroom. I looked at myself in the mirror. I tried to smile, but failed. Splashing some water on my face, I came out.

Diggy caught hold of me as I stepped out.

"Hope you won't do anything that makes me regret inviting you here."

"I won't disturb her. Trust me," I said, and walked to the opposite direction as Diggy went inside the washroom.

I occupied a chair that allowed me to see her. She was joyous, enjoying every moment with her friends. The curves of her lips made me feel happy. I wished I could be the reason for her joy.

Nimisha glanced at me. Nervous, I picked up the menu card and placed it in front of my face, apparently taking a good look before I placed an order for the food. Punit guffawed at the act.

Nimisha tried to ignore me. She faced Vikram and started a conversation that seemed very interesting. I looked at her again, wondering if I could act a little appropriately. But then, who was to decide if my actions were inappropriate? When you're in love, you don't know what's right or wrong. You're just a little cautious about everything you do in front of the person you love.

Nimisha moved a little closer to Diggy and whispered in his ears, "What is he doing here?"

"It's Viraj's birthday. He wanted to spend his day with you," he lowered his tone. "... without disturbing you."

Nimisha considered Diggy's words. A slow smile spread across her lips, and she pushed her chair back. "Excuse me," she said looking at everyone as she left her seat and walked towards my table.

Do you know that feeling when your mind stops working? An electric current flows inside your body. You really don't know whether to stick to your place or run away. I was in the same state when she pulled out the chair and sat in front of me.

"Hi Punit," she greeted my partner who replied in less than nanoseconds. I was sure he was not as immune to her as he tried to show. "Happy birthday, Viraj," she said, as she extended her hand to shake.

The clasp was warm, almost friendly. I thanked her. I never wanted to let go of her soft hands. I wanted to curl my fingers between hers. I wished for her to wish the same.

"So, what are you treating me to?" she asked, with a sparkle in her eyes.

I adjusted the menu which was about to fall from my left hand and passed the same to her with my trembling fingers. "Tell me. What do you want to have?"

"I'm already done with my dinner. Can you buy me some dessert?"

I would have bought all the dreams her eyes had ever dreamt of. I would have bought all the stars from the sky if she would have asked me to. I would have… "Please choose for yourself," I requested.

Punit called a waiter. He placed an order for me without asking my choice, adding an ice cream for Nimisha. He was sure I would have eaten even a plate of grass without any complaint, if Nimisha was siting next to me.

Nimisha came up with topics one after another. I could hardly speak in front of her. Most of the answers to her questions were my smiles. Punit seemed to be enjoying the time as well. She took small bites of the ice cream.

"Know what Viraj… It would not have been bad to have you as my boyfriend." She chuckled, "You really consider and care for the other person's viewpoint. Thank you for respecting my time with my friends. Happy birthday once again. Take care," she smiled as she left her chair.

I pulled out mine to escort her as I saw her friends leaving the table and going out.

"Sit down! Enjoy your meal," she said, making me sit as she placed her hand over my shoulder. It carried a warmth that I had never felt before. "Bye," she stepped away from our table.

"Bye," I said, my mouth half full. I watched her go as she disappeared from my vision. More than a hundred emotions rose in my heart at that moment.

"I will take another treat for this one," Punit said pulling me out of my trance.

"Treat for what?" I looked at him surprised.

"Didn't you notice how she touched your shoulder? Didn't you hear her words?" Punit threw questions rapidly. It irritated me, because I was still living those moments. I didn't want to talk about them, not yet.

I looked at him trying to make out what he meant.

"Man! She is giving you hints. She wants to make you her boyfriend," he added further.

"Eh! What are you saying?" I tried to laugh even though the words had sent me on top of the clouds.

"Trust me," he said stuffing his mouth with some more rice.

We finished our dinner, paid the bill and left the place. All the way to my place, sitting behind Punit, I questioned myself, "*Was Punit's interpretation right? Should I consider her warm gesture as a sign? Does she really want to become my girlfriend? Finally!*"

Presence of your loved ones, even for a few minutes, does enough good to you. You find an unknown energy in your body, joy in your heart and peace in your mind. I could not sleep that night.

Vain Attempt

I wish love could come with a user manual, clearly stating the dos and don'ts for a successful love life. Our life would have been so much easier then. I tried my best to stay out of Nimisha's way, but after my birthday, circumstances were out of my control. My mind always advised me to forget her, but the next moment, she would be standing right in front of me.

In schools and colleges, many of us try not to miss lectures. Not because we take studies seriously, but because the classroom is a place where we can try talking to our crush or a love interest. I was a similar case.

For some time now, even she used to occasionally smile at me. Sometimes she would come to class without a notebook or a pen. She sat behind me. She would ask for couple of sheets of the notebook. I used to give her mine. These were a few times when I could directly look into her eyes. My urge to talk to her grew. I always looked for an opportunity and finally I got one.

"Can I call you tonight if you are not busy with something else?" I said as she was writing her journal.

She looked at me for a moment, then went back to her work. "Don't call me."

"But I want to talk to you."

"You always want to talk to me. But whenever I am in class, you don't have anything to say," she turned the page, without looking at me.

"What's the problem if I call you?"

"It's just that I don't want callers on the phone."

"You wanted to talk on phone when you didn't know who was at the other end." I was losing the calm I had held on to for so long.

"Yes, I did. I wanted to know the person on the other end of the phone."

"What happened after that?"

"I am not interested. Don't you get it?" she asked rudely this time.

"Why should I care about all your whims?" I couldn't control myself from raising my voice.

"Then, don't care."

"I will call you tonight. If you don't answer, I will call tomorrow. If you don't, then day after, until you finally pick up my call." I was not in my senses.

"Be prepared for the consequences."

"I am ready."

She did not reply. She busied herself in writing her assignments, picking up a black pen to underline a couple of words.

"Why can't we be good friends?" I asked

"Because I don't trust you."

"What should I do to change that?"

"If you want to talk to me, talk to me in the classroom…" she stopped as Diggy entered.

He sat on a desk facing us. I did not want to create a scene. She stood from her bench to walk towards Diggy. I wanted to stop her, but all I could do was just say the words, "Will call you at night."

She didn't reply. Diggy looked at me. I packed my rucksack and was about to leave the class for a practical.

"Nimisha, you go. I will be in the lab in just a few minutes," he instructed Nimisha. "Viraj, can you wait a while? I need to talk to you." Diggy turned to me.

"Yes, tell me."

"Have you forgotten? She had kind of forgiven you. Why are you interfering in her life again?" He came straight to the point.

I was sizzling. Even I had thought, things had turned in my favour and had attempted sharing my wishes with her. Now, it was going downhill again, "Who are you to interfere in my life?"

"I am her good friend."

"Then please, be a good friend to her. Don't try to order me." I picked my rucksack from the desk and left the room, banging the door behind me.

There live two personalities within me. One good, the other bad. Every day I wake up, I force the bad to go to sleep and good to accompany me. Most days I win, but sometimes, I do fail. I felt really upset speaking to a good friend like that. I spent the next two hours thinking about the discussion I had with Nimisha that afternoon. I was turning into a villain for her, I concluded.

"I agree to everything," I said to Nimisha when we met after labs.

She did not say a word. Her smiling face was enough to say that she was happy to hear that from me. I called Diggy in the evening. He asked me to meet him in the back market. I told him what happened after labs. He tried to console me, but wasn't much help to me or my pain.

Punit's encouragement on my birthday had led me to bring up the subject with her. And it had not gone as I wanted it to go. She was still far from me, if not farther. Nothing seemed right.

I didn't meet any of my friends. I didn't spend time watching movies or playing games. I stopped going to the mess to eat. The hair on my head and face was crying for a trim. My body was growing weak. After I had given up on food, I started forgetting even water. I was lost, and followed just one routine. Wake up, get ready for college, look at her all day in class, not utter a single word to anyone, return home and finally sleep so that I could continue with my routine the next day. Not a single change.

That day I tried to eat, but couldn't. It had been four days since anything had gone inside my mouth. I didn't even care to get some liquid in my belly. The very next day, I went close to her seat and said, "I can't continue my life like this."

"How did you manage for so long?" She had a question for me. I stayed silent.

Vishwa, Vikram and Ankur surrounded my desk. She tried to ask them to stop. However, they were angry, seeing me falling back to my old ways. I had an argument with them. They provoked, discussed, fought. I finally had to leave the class just to preserve my sanity.

"What happened?" Punit asked as he saw me coming out of the classroom.

"Nothing," I said.

"Just tell me what they said?"

I recounted the incident. We were at the entrance of Sachai Mata Temple. He said, "Let's go inside for a few moments. You will feel good."

"You are free to go. I will wait for you outside the gate."

"Why?"

"You know that I never visit temples."

"Start now. Everything will be fine."

How could I explain the relation between the supreme power of the universe and me? God and I had an old enmity. I had dreamt of several things in my life and God had tried his best to never give them to me.

"What are you thinking? Come fast," he almost shouted at me.

I looked at the building that housed god. I had tried almost everything to convince Nimisha. Nothing had worked so far. Maybe, this was the last thing I could do to get her – fold my hands in front of my enemy. The temple was decorated for the occasion of Navratra. I took off my shoes, washed my hands, touched the first stair of the temple and went in. It was a lovely temple, shining from one end to another. I clanged the bell hard and moved towards the idol of the goddess. I folded my hands and closed my eyes reverently. The goddess appeared in front of me.

"Hello goddess," I said. "I've not cared to worship you for long now. Still I need a favour from you."

"You did not care about me," she said with a smiling face. "Why should I listen to you or your request?"

"I promise you that I will be your good son. I will visit you regularly if you fulfill my wishes today."

"And, if I don't?"

"Then, too. I will come to you, visit you every week here as long as I live in this city."

"What can I do for you?"

"You know what I am here for."

The goddess smiled again.

"Please give me at least one thing that I want in my life," I requested with my hands folded and head bent.

"Humans don't care about all that they have. They are always greedy to get more and more," the goddess said.

"Even if I am greedy, just give me a few precious moments so that I can talk to her."

"I can't give everyone what they want."

"At least do something for me."

"I will do the best for you. Trust me."

I opened my eyes the next morning, pushing myself off the bed. My legs were fixed to the surface. I couldn't balance myself. I plonked on the floor and stayed motionless. Punit rushed towards me as he heard the noise in the room.

"Is everything fine?" Punit asked, helping me back on my bed.

"I don't know." I was worried too.

"What do you mean?"

"I don't know if I am well. I feel weak," I said as I reclined against the wall.

"Let's visit a doctor."

We reached the college's hospital in another hour. Dr Chouhan was ready to examine me.

"When did you last have a meal?" The lady doctor asked.

"Five days ago." I lowered my eyes.

"Get on that," she pointed towards a weighing machine.

"Forty-seven…" I tried to push myself hard on the machine so that it could make some change in its reading. It failed.

"Come up here," she called me back. "You should be much heavier than what you are now."

I nodded my head in agreement.

"What are you doing with your life?"

"Doctor, I was fasting duringNavratra," I said after thinking a little. God knew, impressing Nimisha was more difficult than impressing the goddess herself.

"If you are not able to handle it, you should not fast."

"Sorry, I am helpless."

She left her chair, thought for a moment and walked out of her cabin. She might have gone out looking for a patient who could be cured easily. Love is a disease whose symptoms make your life a living hell, yet you never want to get out of it, nor can you find the right medicines to cure it.

"Come along with me," she called me when she returned. I followed her.

I was taken to a huge cabin with medals in all corners. An old doctor sat on his chair. He instructed me to sit down.

"Until you eat, we can't cure you," the old doctor said, adjusting his thick spectacles, looking at the half filled prescription mentioning my health issues on the table.

"I can't eat. I am fasting."

"There is no cure to hunger," he looked at me again.

I didn't say a word.

"Should I call your principal and say that one of your students has no more interest in studies?"

I shook my head.

"Then, eat something. You are just a kid."

"I am extremely sorry." I was fast losing the energy in me. All I wanted was to lie down somewhere.

The doctor didn't say anything. Dr Chouhan asked me to go to her cabin and stay there. The two doctors discussed my case for a few minutes. Dr Chouhan returned soon.

"Are your classes going on?" she inquired.

"Yes."

"Do you have anything important going on in your college?"

"Not really."

"We need to admit you in the hospital. If you can't eat, we will have to push some saline into your body."

I was surprised.

"When?"

"Now." Her answer astonished me.

Within no time, I was shifted from the chair in her cabin to a bed in the hospital.

The narrow bed was covered with a clean white bedsheet. There was a matching white pillow. A small table was on my left, near the pillow. My right side had a small stool meant for visitors.

"You need to bring these from the medical shop downstairs," the nurse said as she passed a slip to Punit. He looked at the slip and its contents.

"Call someone who can be with you here. I have to get the medicines," he said without looking at me.

"Give a call to Nikhil," I passed my mobile to Punit.

He called Nikhil, who came in a few minutes and Punit went downstairs to bring the injections that I needed. Nikhil walked around my bed, twice. He then sat on the stool next to me.

"I really feel sad that you are here," Nikhil said resting his cheek on his hand.

"*If you feel so sad, why don't you take my place in this bed?*" I thought.

Punit came with two plastic bottles that were required to provide saline to my body. There were vials of liquids, syringes to suck out my blood and other stuff, the mere sight of which was ruining my health further.

"Here it is," he handed the plastic bag to the nurse.

She placed an IV stand near my bed and left the room with the bag Punit had given her. When I saw her next, she held a syringe larger than the size of my palm. The needle tip glistened. I stood helpless in front of the sword of Tipu Sultan preparing to stab my body.

"The doctor said they just wanted to administer some saline," I was terrified.

"We also need to get a few tests done," she was unmoved.

I am not a dead body. Why do they need to experiment everything on me?

"Will you insert the whole needle?" I asked her trying to come to terms with the size of the thing.

"No, just a little. We need to take some blood," she said and held my right hand.

"You mean..."

"Look there," she pointed to my left.

I looked to my left for a moment.

"Oh… Bitch!" I mumbled as the needle jabbed my right arm. I winced in pain.

"I heard that. Keep this pressed here," she said as she pressed the cotton on the affected area.

I pressed the cotton to my biceps. The syringe was filled with my dark red blood. *Does she even know how long it takes for that much blood to form in the body? If each test required this much blood, soon my body will be bloodless and will contain only saline, provided they put it in a few minutes.* The nurse left, holding the syringe in her hand.

"Why are you behaving like a kid?" Nikhil asked.

"I am not."

"So, what is this?"

"I hope at least you can understand me."

He did not reply. The nurse came back with the bottle of saline water and another syringe. She put the saline water on the table beside me and came to me with the injection.

"Do you need to take more blood?"

"No, I just need to inject."

I was injected several times. A thin transparent pipe moved from the saline bottle to my left hand, making my body cold. I lay calmly on my bed.

"I need to go to my room. I have some work in college," Punit said.

"I too have to get my journals checked," Nikhil said.

"You both let me die here in this condition. Enjoy your classes. Can't either of you stay?" I asked adjusting my pillow.

"I will be back as soon as I can," Nikhil said.

"Call someone who can be here till I complete my work," Punit said.

"Whom?" Nikhil thought for a moment.

"Call someone who can make me laugh. I am dying with pain here," I said as I closed my eyes.

"Just put a mirror in front of yourself and you will laugh a lot," Nikhil mocked.

Punit left for his flat. Nikhil stayed for a while. After texting Diggy to visit the hospital, he left for college too. I didn't know when I fell asleep.

"He is dying in the hospital. Can't you go and see him once?" Punit was almost shouting at Nimisha as she studied the notice board outside the Training and Placement Department.

"He will be alright. Don't worry," she said.

"He hasn't eaten… for God knows how many days."

"She can't visit every patient in the hospital who stops eating," Vishwa said as he joined them.

"Shut up," Punit screamed at Vishwa. When your friend is in pain, you will do anything that can relieve him. That's the rule of true friendship. "He is not just anyone. He is our classmate."

"Sorry, I can't meet him. Why don't you try to make him understand?" she said as she left.

"What will..."

"Please, I am getting late for my lunch. Bye," she said cutting him short.

"*Oh God! How did you create this world with so many varieties of people? There is one who is dying in hospital without having food for days and there is this girl, who can't be late for her lunch,*" Punit thought.

I woke up after a short nap. Punit, Diggy, Nikhil and Sahil surrounded me. I felt uncomfortable as so many people were getting disturbed because of me.

"I spoke to Nimisha. She doesn't care about you. Not even a pinch. Eat properly and get out of here," Punit said.

"I can't."

"Don't behave like a kid. We have our semester exams two months later. If you don't eat, your health will deteriorate further," Nikhil said.

"Just bring her here for a few minutes," I sobbed.

"Only he can help you now," Punit mumbled, pointing at Diggy.

"Please, is this a bullshit show put up to get her here?" Diggy was angry.

"If my pain seems fake, you should have chosen not to come."

"I can't help you, Viraj. She doesn't listen to me. Otherwise, I'd have tried," he said, disappointed.

"Can I be alone? I beg of you." Tears rolled down my eyes.

"For whom are you wasting these teardrops? For the one who doesn't even think about you?" Punit yelled.

"Please," I pleaded again.

They left after a few minutes. I closed my eyes and thought about the girl I had always dreamt of. No matter how much pain the person you love gives you, she will still appear an angel to you. I was lost in the fairy tale with her in my dreams once again.

"If you don't eat, I will throw you out of this bed." Punit shouted as I looked at him.

"Try that too," I said, emotionless.

"Why are you doing this?"

"I am defeated."

"For whom are you wasting your life?"

"You know her."

"Can't you live for people who care about you? Who sent you here, your parents who had dreams for you?"

He was making a point.

"Can we go out of this place? I want to leave this bed for a while," I said trying to sit on the bed.

"If you promise me you will eat something when we are back." He held my left hand and arranged the pillow so that I could rest against the wall.

"I will try my best."

"Wait here. I will ask the nurse." Punit left the room. I touched my face. The tears had dried on my cheeks.

"The nurse has allowed you to just walk here. She instructed me not to go far from your bed as shifts are to change in another fifteen minutes," Punit said as he helped me getting down from the bed.

I put my bare feet on the cold floor. I felt some energy within me. Maybe because of the saline. We walked near the lift. I pressed its button.

"Stop. She did not allow you to go out."

"Do you have the bike keys? We will be back soon," I said as we entered the lift. We got out of the hospital and finally out of our campus.

Punit brought two food packets from Jain mess when we returned to the hospital. I was feeling much better.

"Where were you?" the nurse shouted at Punit. The shift had changed.

"We were just walking on the ground floor."

"Don't you know doctors come for a round after a shift change?"

"No. When will he be back?" Punit asked, surprised.

"He's already left. He will only be coming tomorrow now."

She took my temperature and my blood pressure. "Everything is normal," she informed us.

I sighed at her words. She shook the thermometer to bring it to the base reading. Punit and I were talking about journals to be completed when I saw a lovely lady looking at me. She was a nurse. She came towards us.

"So, you are an engineer?" she asked me.

"Not really. I am a second year engineering student."

"I'd better say to-be-engineer then," she said and smiled.

Her smile was infectious. I could not control myself from smiling back.

"You know… I too wished to become an engineer. But it was not meant to be."

"Why?" I asked her, curious.

"The fee is higher in engineering colleges as compared to nursing. That's why my father asked me to join this profession and I did."

"Thus, you are helping here, caring for patients in a hospital." I smiled.

"Yes, I joined here as an intern last month," she smiled back.

"Oh, am so sorry. Would you like to sit?" I offered making a little place on my bed.

"No, we are not allowed to sit and talk with patients," she said with a smile.

"Okay."

"You are quite lucky to be an engineer." Her eyes sparkled. While others crave for it, how many of us appreciate the opportunities we get?

"You too are extremely lucky. Getting blessings from so many patients and their families." I smiled.

"I should see those patients now," she smiled regretfully, as if she didn't want to leave.

I looked at her chest. Her name tag clearly mentioned her name, 'Sheetal Gandhi.'

"You can have my number if you want," I said. She didn't say anything but waited for me to narrate the number. "Punit, write it down and give it to her please," I instructed Punit who was listening to us.

He handed her a slip after jotting my number on it. She left waving and smiling at me.

"Why did you give your number to her?" Punit attacked like a storm.

"There should be someone to talk to on the phone after Nimisha," I joked.

Punit laughed out loud. I tried to eat that night and was able to have two chapatis. I could not eat any more than that. That night I closed my eyes, saying the last prayer of the day. "Oh God, with every sunrise over the years, the sun has never failed to bring with it a new, fresh and promising day, I wish every dawn to leave me a teeny weeny bit wiser and hopefully a more mature creature."

Laila

Someone has rightly said: "The best way to forget a girl is to fill your brain with another." But the efforts were in vain.

Many nights of tear-stained pillows is the cold truth for people with broken hearts. Another undeniable truth is a few nights of drunken revelry and broken hearts mend. Also it is common belief that cure for a broken heart is another woman.

Tear-stained pillows suit girls. Drinking wasn't my habit. I was left only with the last option.

Punit and I sat in my room. The time for submission of journals was fast approaching. Guys who hadn't completed file work the entire semester had started crowding my place, for journals. Utsav was among them.

"Hi! How are you?" Utsav entered my room, loosening his shoelaces, getting comfortable.

"Good. What about you?" I smiled at my friend.

"Rough times!"

"Can I be of help?" I inquired, aware of what he needed.

"EDC journal," he didn't waste any time in coming to the point.

"Yes…"

Utsav's ringing phone cut me off, before I could fully agree.

"Shh..." he touched his lips with his fingers, signaling us to stay quiet.

He put the phone on speaker.

"What are you doing sweetheart?" a melodious voice asked.

We could overhear everything she said.

"I am at my friend's place," Utsav replied.

"Hope the friend is not a girl."

Punit and I grinned.

"Of course not darling," Utsav crooned.

"When will you meet me?"

"I will give you a ring before I come."

"You are forgetting something," she giggled.

"What?"

"Muah... Muaaahhhh... Muaahhhh." Her kisses floated in the air.

Utsav glanced embarrassingly at our smiling faces. "My friends can hear you."

"What?" She sounded shocked.

"Yeah, the phone is on speaker," Utsav explained.

"Are you stupid? Why did you put me on speaker?" Her voice was angry.

"My ears are aching because of using earphones for long duration," he touched his right ear.

"Stupid guy!"

Utsav disconnected the phone. "Stupid girl."

"This was stupidity? Demand does decrease with supply. If only..." I smirked looking at Punit.

"Where did you get that sweet-voiced girl?" Punit asked.

"What do you mean by where did I get her? She proposed to me last month," Utsav informed casually.

Utsav was the quintessential dude – fair complexion, adorable smile, funky hairstyle. He owned a shiny Pulsar which he rode around the city. Had he only been a foot taller, he could have given any model a run for his money.

"Does she have an unattached friend?" I enquired mischievously.

"I do believe one of her friends broke up recently. Hopefully she is single," Utsav answered, genuinely.

"The question isn't her relationship status. The question is…" I sniggered, "Is she ready to mingle?"

"Not sure. Wait a minute," he said punching some buttons on the mobile. A moment later, he disconnected the call.

"Do you want to use my phone?" Punit offered his mobile to Utsav.

"No. Have plenty of talk-time in mine, but then what's the point of having a rich girlfriend?" He winked.

Less than a minute and his mobile rang. He moved to the next room. We awaited his return silently.

"Jot down," Utsav scrolled his phonebook.

He dictated a number. I saved it in my phone. He took the journal and was about to leave.

"What did you say to your girlfriend that she gave the number so easily?" I couldn't believe it had been so easy for him. I had had to go to such lengths to get one number. It had taken months.

"I told her you are the best guy in our batch. Helpful and a good friend."

"And what is the name of this girl who will fall for these qualities?" Punit asked.

"Laila."

What's more difficult – to forget the one you loved, or to not forget her? Life had come to a standstill. I wasn't able to forget the girl. Crossing each day in the calendar had become a habit. I celebrated any day which went without thinking about her and immediately fell back into the pit that echoed with only one word, Nimisha.

No one was happy with my condition. Not my friends, not me. I needed to forget her, once and for all. And soon. One especially depressing day, I called Laila for the first time.

"Hi Laila!" I said as soon as she picked up my call.

"Who is this?"

"This is Viraj, Utsav's friend."

"Oh!"

"I hope I didn't call at an awkward time. Were you doing something important?" The fear that seized me when I called Nimisha was coming back.

"Playing Ludo with my cousins," she answered, like a kid.

Her gentle reply made me lose all my fear in seconds.

"Really?" I guffawed, "You need to continue?"

"No. My cousin will play for me."

As soon as I found out she was willing to talk to me, a silence fell. The most difficult thing for a boy is to initiate a topic of discussion when speaking to a girl for the first time. It's worse if they haven't met face to face. It was something Nimisha had often felt when I called her.

"Do you know why I called you?" I tried.

"For some good bonding, Utsav said…" she spoke like a child, again.

"Hope we can be good friends." I wasn't very hopeful though.

"The better I get to know you, the better friends we will be."

"I have two eyes, two ears, a nose, a mouth, two hands, two legs and a lot of other stuff. Now you know everything about me," I smiled, tickled by my reply.

"What? Nothing unique…." She sounded disappointed.

"If I would have been a boy with unique features like one eye, one ear, two noses, two mouths, would you still like to be my friend?"

"At least you have a good sense of humour," she giggled.

"Now, it's your turn."

"I study at Singhad College. I believe Utsav told you that."

"He told me, you are his girlfriend's friend. And... you are single," I chuckled.

"I broke up with Shrey last month," Her voice turned serious.

"Hey, I didn't want to upset you. I was just..."

"You didn't upset me. His brother did." She continued further, "He saw Shrey and me somewhere and informed their mother about me. His mother made him swear he wouldn't continue his relationship with me. He is Sindhi, I am a Muslim. Different religions, you know?"

"No, I don't know. What I have come to know in this short chat that you are really a very sweet girl."

"I feel the same about you. I will wait for your next call," Laila was definitely smiling.

I wasn't sure if I would ever call her again. It was a dilemma. *Was I doing the right thing? Was I not returning to the same path I had travelled earlier? Where would this path take me this time?* I did not have an answer. *Should I call her again? Maybe yes. Maybe no.* Too many questions. But sometimes, you don't look for answers. You leave them to be answered by time. I let my phone drop to the table.

Two days later, I called her again.

She was breathing heavily when she picked up my call. She had been playing kho kho with her cousins.

"Er! I disturb you every time you are playing something," I said, hearing about the ongoing game.

"You are not really disturbing me. You call me anytime these days, I will be found playing something or the other. My studies begin just before the exams. And there is plenty of time for that," she sounded more breathless with each word.

These statements always gave me the feeling that students had no life. They spent most of it awaiting the day when exams would begin or end.

"By the way, you talk like a friend of mine in Delhi," Laila observed. Her breathing had stabilized. She sounded normal now.

"And what does this friend do?"

"I don't really know. We have spoken a couple of times. Generally we chat over the internet."

"Tell me more about you Laila." I was curious.

"There is nothing much to share. What do you like? And what you don't?"

"I like things that an insane person likes."

"And, what sort of things are they?"

"There is a broad spectrum. I like going out and getting wet in the rain. I enjoy the rain."

"Your nose must also rain all the time, then, right?" she said sweetly.

"Not anymore. Earlier it used to," I answered genuinely. "But with time I have toughened."

"What else is insane?"

"Every night at one, in my college, people find me holding a bottle of Mountain Dew," I continued.

"But it's so cold in Pune."

"Yes, the colder the weather, the better chilled ice cream and cold drinks taste." I smiled.

"You are a freak," she shrieked.

I could hear someone calling her in the background. She requested that we speak later.

"When will you tell me about yourself? You must find time and call me," I said.

"Absolutely. Bye, got to go," she disconnected the call.

The beep rattled my eardrums. I was moving the same path. The path that had led me to destruction earlier.

There's a truth about every heart. No matter how many times it breaks, no matter how many times it is hurt, it is always ready to give someone another chance.

My heart was ready to give someone another chance, unwilling to understand that it might cause trouble for me again.

Laila too liked talking to me!

Her missed calls became a routine, for my mobile. And my mobile would dial her number like a maniac the very next moment.

Our discussions encompassed a spectrum. We shared everything. My night outs at Banjara Hills, cold coffee at Durga Cafe at one in the night, to her mischief of mixing beer in her puppy's milk. She laughed uncontrollably while explaining how her puppy acted after having beer-milk.

Even the smallest of things happening in her life found regular passage to my ears. Her quarrels with her brother, her excitement about her would-be-sister-in-law; each and every bit was a part of our conversations.

That day, in keeping with the routine, I came out of the reading hall to answer a missed call from her number.

The first words were, "Why did you take so long? Who were you busy with? Answer me!"

"I was studying in the reading hall," I settled on the stairs to the third floor.

"You are busy studying every time I call. What about other things in life?" She sounded hyper energetic.

"I do a number of things. You know all about them."

"No college, no studies. I am bored with this life. I want to enjoy life…with someone," she paused momentarily. "What else?"

My mind whirred!

"Is this Laila? Am I talking to the same girl? 'What Else?' was my question when she would stop talking. How did it transfer to her? Why were topics escaping me, and I was left with nothing to say? It was usually her status," my mind ticked doubtfully.

"Who are you?" The next second, my mouth matched my brain's tone.

"Laila! Are you alright?"

"No, you aren't Laila. Your voice is similar, but I have been talking to her for some time now. I know you're not Laila. May I know who is this?"

She hesitated for a moment, then replied, "This is Aaliya, Laila's cousin." She greeted me anew, "Hello!"

"Aaliya… I am hearing your name for the first time. What made you talk to me?" I scratched my head, curious.

"Laila was busy. I saw you calling, so picked up the phone."

"What do you do Aaliya?"

"Study. Bachelors in Fashion Technology," she informed with pride as if the future of the industry depended on her.

My mind was still in doubt. A background voice said, "What are you doing? Give it to me."

"Are you really Laila's cousin? She has told me about everyone in her family, but your name never came up."

"Man! You think too much. Fine, you caught me," she confessed.

"Finally!" I took a triumphant breath.

"This is Soniya, Utsav's girlfriend," she giggled.

"Oh… hi." I attempted a smile.

"What's up dude?"

"You made me bleed sweat! For a second I thought I was talking to her mother."

"Not so fast dude. Years before you reach there," she joked.

"Very funny. Could you please ask Laila to speak to me?" I requested, uncomfortable talking to my friend's girl.

"You talk to her every day. Try me today," she sounded like she really wanted to.

"What shall we talk about? I don't know you," I explained my hesitation.

"Why? Someday you spoke to Laila in the same manner."

"You don't get it," I was getting uncomfortable with her persistence. "It was different. She was a girl…"

"I too am a girl," she said indignantly, cutting me short.

"But, Utsav's girlfriend." That should clarify it, I thought.

"Hey, you won't blab to Utsav, right?" She sounded concerned. "Me chatting you up…" she asked.

"Why? What's the problem?"

"He gets jealous if I talk to a boy. Jealous!" she emphasized.

"Then you should not be talking to me." I understood Utsav's point.

"Sometimes I feel like talking to new people. New boys. It's not fair that I should not, just because he said so, right?" She needed me to agree with her. How complicated is the heart? We could have the entire world's love from a person, yet we do not fail to look for something that we don't have.

"But if your boyfriend does not want you to, then me talking to you is wrong," I offered my opinion.

"Ignore that. You won't tell him we spoke?"

"I don't lie to my friends, ever!" I emphasized.

"Hey please," she sounded desperate. "If you tell him, he will break up with me."

"Okay, I will try my best."

"Thank you. Now tell me. What's keeping you occupied?"

"My semester exams. Can I speak to Laila now?" I reminded her.

"You are so desperate. Can't you talk to me?"

"I can. But…" I trailed, not having an answer. I did not want to. I just wanted to hear Laila.

"But what? Think of me as your girlfriend for a day," she chuckled.

"What!" I was shocked.

"You heard me."

"You are embarrassing me." Really! Didn't she know the bro code?

"Why are you like that? Utsav said you are a Baniya. Me too. Let's get married," she offered.

I was speechless.

"We won't have any complications, same community," she spoke as if she was giving it a lot of thought.

I finally said, "What about Utsav?" How could girls take matters like these so lightly?

"He is smart. He will get another girl."

"After that?"

"After marriage?" She paused, as if thinking. "We will have kids. At least a dozen, we will make our own cricket team," she grinned.

"Are you out of your senses? You know how much a dozen means?" I opened my arms wide apart, trying to gather our future kids in them. Failing.

"Okay. How about five?" she asked my opinion.

"Five," I considered with difficulty

"Yes, one will be a doctor, next engineer, third one, an architect…" She had made the important choices of our kids' lives.

"What about the other two?" I asked.

"Should I decide for all? You will be the father. Why don't you think about their future?" She scolded me like a seasoned wife.

"*All right, mother of my kids, forgive me. I will shoulder my responsibilities,*" I thought deeply. "Please pass the phone to Laila."

"You are behaving as if you are trapped in net of our relationship like a dying fish," she scolded me this time.

"Hey, will you stop this?"

"No, I won't."

"Please, I beg of you, forgive me."

"I like a fluttering fish trapped in net, destined to be fried in hot oil. Yummy!" She laughed out loudly, not at all like a gentle girl.

"Oh, lovely mom of twelve children, forgive me today," I almost folded my hands in request.

"Not so easy. Get down on your knees, hands behind you, face hung down in apology. Show me some tears. Then, I will." She giggled, enjoying the thought of punishment she meted.

"Please Soniya, it's about time."

"Okay. I forgive you, but answer me truthfully. Do you love Laila?"

Another bomb explosion! I had lost count, of how many she had thrown at me in single day. This girl was turning out to be a serial killer.

I did not have an answer. She had no idea what she had asked.

"Don't worry. She is not here," she assured me.

"I like her… but don't love her," I answered truthfully. What I thought was the truth.

"What do you mean by that?"

"It means, of course she is a dear friend, but not my girlfriend. Is that clear enough?" I wanted the conversation to end quickly.

"Is it going to remain so, or would you consider the next step?" she asked in a low tone.

"I believe, it should continue like this," I was not ready for another heart attachment.

"Why? Don't you like her?"

"I do, but..." I trailed.

"But what? Is her being a Muslim an issue?"

"No. I don't think so."

"Then, what is it?" Her tone was challenging.

"Look. She is from a conservative family. If I take the next step, I know she will get in trouble."

Soniya nodded.

"Can I talk to Laila now? Please. I insist."

"You fried up fish," she had the last word, as she finally passed the phone to Laila.

"Hi!"

Finally, I heard a voice I was comfortable with. "Your friend is amazing. How can she trouble someone to such an extent?" I asked Laila.

"She has mastered that art. Some people take pleasure in irritating people all the time," she commented, gnashing her teeth at Soniya.

"What else?"

"Nothing. You say."

And it continued for another half an hour.

Soniya called me several times after that. Thankfully, she was calmer than the first time.

Sometimes she would sing in her lovely voice, '*Khaiyke paan Benaras wala*' and so on. Soon, I made another friend in Soniya. We exchanged numbers. However, she instructed me not to call her as Utsav could find out. She called me, and occasionally I used to reply with an SMS.

"When are you coming to meet us?" she asked.

"Whenever your friend wishes."

"She wants to meet you, but hesitates in saying so," Soniya replied, as if in pain.

From the quarrel that followed I understood, Laila was pulling her hair.

"Then it is in the almighty's hand."

"Can I come to see you at your college?" Soniya asked.

"Have you lost your mind? There are so many friends in college. What will they say? And what about Utsav?" I raised my eyebrows, which she could not see.

"He is going out of station to attend a relative's wedding, I guess. Next Tuesday. We can meet up then." She had it all sorted.

"Okay, I can consider it. Not in college though. Some other place. Far."

"Oh, the coward fish!"

"Will let you know the place soon. But, will it be possible for all of us to meet?" I asked her.

"All, including…?"

"Laila, you and me."

"Don't worry, I will bring her along," Soniya promised.

"I will SMS the time."

We did not talk for the next two days. Nor did any of her messages reach my phone.

I shut my book, fed up, banging it lightly on the table. I picked up my phone to set the alarm.

Soniya had texted.

'What?' I replied.

'We were to meet this week,' came her reply.

I wondered if I should have called her to campus.

'When do you want to meet?' I asked anyway.

'Tomorrow,' she responded.

'I have classes,' I informed her.

'Bunk them,' came her reply.

'Will see,' I replied.

'Let me know.'

Then the phone went silent.

I set the alarm, took a sip from the bottle on the table, and switched off the lights.

Just Can't

We reached INOX sharp at 4 p.m. A large poster of *Namastey London* was mounted on the wall of the gigantic building. There wasn't much crowd outside the building, though a few groups were scattered near the ticket counter. Others stood waiting as the previous movie show was still going on.

"I think the girls are still inside enjoying the movie. What should we do?" I asked Punit. We were standing near the ticket counter.

"We did not come here to look at posters. We came to meet them, so we will wait. Give one of them a call," Punit said gawking at a girl in a mini dress.

It's not appreciated when you call someone in the middle of a show. Any disturbance after paying hundreds to get these movie tickets is not tolerated. However, I dialled Soniya's number. She picked up after the sixth ring.

"Hi! Where are you?" I asked.

"Watching the movie. Where are you?" I could hear the distant rumble of the movie dialogues on the other end of the phone.

"I am waiting for you at McDonald's downstairs. How long will you take?" McDonald's on the ground floor was less crowded at that moment.

"I think it will take about half an hour," she replied.

"Come out, yaar. I hate waiting."

"I came to enjoy the movie. Why should I leave it in the middle?" She kept her point.

"How many times have you seen it already?"

"It's the third time as far as I remember," she smirked.

"Then just come out, please."

"Order something in the meantime. We will be out in fifteen minutes. Bye," she said and disconnected the phone.

"She will be out soon," I said, rolling up my sleeves, getting comfortable.

"How much money do you have in your wallet?" Punit asked.

"Fifty or sixty bucks."

"That's all? Before coming out, didn't you remember, we are going to meet girls today?" Punit mocked.

"I came here to meet them. Not to spend money on them." I gave a disinterested look.

"If you want girls to spend money in the following outings, you have to spend well the first time. Few things are unsaid laws, man." His theories about girls were never-ending. He turned towards the exit.

"Let me know which law says your bike must be getting serviced when we need to go to various places." Punit's bike was at the service station and we were walking or taking buses to every other place.

"That's good. If you are lucky, who knows, someone will give you a ride on her scooter." He smiled.

I withdrew a few hundreds and came out of the ATM. My phone rang.

"Where are you?" Soniya asked.

"I came to withdraw some money."

"If you didn't have money, you could have borrowed some from me. Why was it necessary to go? You had said you were waiting..."

"I was bound by some laws," I offered lamely.

"What? Anyway, come fast! We left the movie's climax for you, and you are not even here."

"Just give us five minutes." We crossed the road to reach the pavement.

"Don't run. Let them wait," Punit said.

Ten minutes later, Punit and I scanned every corner of McDonald's for four girls waiting for two guys. We didn't find them.

"Where are you?" I called up Soniya, again.

"Can you come down to CCD, MG Road, please?"

"What the hell? Are you all crazy? We almost ran to reach here and now you are asking me to run to MG Road."

"Please, please, please... someone who knows me was there at INOX. I could have got into trouble if he saw me with you. Hope you can understand."

"Oh, we will need to take an auto to reach there. You make me spend so much," I spoke my pain in a joking manner.

"Take the money from me. Fine?" she said half rudely.

"That's so kind of you. I would be pleased to." I angrily disconnected the call.

Guys, understand... girls twirl us around. They take advantage of us emotionally, financially, every which way that serves their purpose. We know what is happening with us is wrong, but we remain helpless victims. So now we were frantically rushing to find an auto which could give us a ride to MG Road.

Three girls sat on a red sofa facing a huge television. Some music channel was playing the latest Bollywood blockbuster. The rectangular glass table was occupied by their handkerchiefs and mobiles. One among them stood up when we got down from the auto.

"Viraj?" The girl approached me.

I nodded.

"Hi, I am Shreya," she said. "Come over there," she pointed towards a table where the girls sat.

Punit and I reached the table, the girls surrounded us. First meetings are always like walking on hot coals. I was walking carefully, absolutely confused, as to who among them was Laila.

"Hi! I am Soniya," one said.

"Sweta," the other waved.

"I am Viraj and this is my friend Punit," I said as we pulled up our chairs. I looked in all directions for Laila. I could not find her.

"Laila is on the phone. She will be back in two minutes. Look, here she comes," Soniya read my searching eyes and pointed to a girl.

Laila wore a light brown kameez and a blue salwar. Her dupatta had colors of brown, white and blue. Her long, light brown hair was mostly open. A hair pin tried its best to keep the hair from falling on her face. She wore long golden earrings that looked nice on her and matched the corners of her dupatta. She had a black rucksack by the legs of the chair on which she adjusted herself.

"Hi," she said.

I raised my hand in greeting. Punit smiled at her.

"Can we order something before we get chatting?" Soniya asked.

I nodded.

The girls discussed some foreign names among themselves. I didn't understand a single name. I was coming to CCD for the second time. The first time when I was there, I had concentrated on the cricket match on their giant TV. I believe CCDs and other cafeterias are the show off places of the rich. It was surely out of my league.

"Frappe?" Soniya asked.

I was hearing the name for the first time. Some alien must have named it. Three among the four girls agreed to the same. Perhaps, all coffee tastes good when cute girls offer it to you.

"Ya ya," I avoided repeating the alien name. A wrong pronunciation could get me giggled upon by the girls.

Punit nodded too. It is tough to disagree with sweet girls. I was dead sure Punit was also hearing the name for the first time. Soniya handed a few hundred rupee notes to Shreya as she went to order for us.

"Good to see that you both are in matching clothes," Soniya giggled. "Are you in your college uniform?"

"You must have seen Utsav several times in the same dress?" I picked up the menu card lying on the table, trying to act like I was studying the names of the coffees.

"Never." Haughtily she adjusted her handbag which was falling to her right.

"For wearing a college uniform, you need to go to the college first," Punit grinned.

The girls laughed out loudly. Soniya's confidence shook a little.

"You both bunked your classes to meet us?" Soniya asked after some time.

"For the first time," I said.

"You could have changed your clothes before you came to meet us," Soniya suggested.

"I told him to change." Punit gave me a dirty look.

"If you did, why didn't you change yourself?" She smiled as if he had failed to show off his intelligence.

"I didn't allow him. I would have had to go to my flat to change. My brother would know that I bunked my class and we were going to some other place. And I didn't want that, so I didn't allow him either."

Five large glasses with beautiful liquids occupied our table along with a cup of hot coffee. They called it kappacheeno, I guess. I waited for girls to start with their drinks. I picked the glass last.

Laila took first few sips from her glass with the straw, but later put it on the tray. She drank the entire glass in the next minute. A white moustache ran below her nose. She looked cute. A pink tongue came out to lick the falling drops of the coffee.

"Isn't this place crowded?" Soniya asked.

"It's one of the most happening places in the city," Punit placed the glass on the table.

"Could we go to some other place?"

Punit looked at me. I nodded.

We stepped out of CCD and followed the girls. They stopped at various stalls that were in the path of CCD and the parking area.

"They should not have so many one way roads. We have to walk a lot," Soniya complained. She picked up a pair of earrings sold by a road-side vendor.

Girls are the most confusing creations of god. They pick up an item, hold it against the part where it is to be worn, look at themselves in the mirror and ask, 'This looks nice, *na*?' Seeing their innocently hopeful smile awaiting approval, even if you hate it, you will definitely say, 'It looks great'. The same moment, they will keep it back, make a sad face and say, 'Not so good.'

I looked around for Laila. She was lagging behind as her rucksack kept falling from her shoulders. I waited till she could reach us.

"Shall I take it?" I offered. She hesitated.

"Take it, but don't run away with it," Soniya joked.

"Don't worry," I said pulling the rucksack from her hand.

We walked another five minutes to reach the place where hundreds of scooters were parked in queues.

"Who among you knows to drive well?" Soniya asked, holding scooter keys in her hand.

I looked at Punit. Soniya threw her scooter keys to him. He smiled as he caught the keys.

"Drive slow. Wait at Carnival, Koregaon Park. Hope you will like the place," Soniya said as she paid the parking guy.

Punit and I reached Carnival before the others. A large wooden house was surrounded by trees of different sizes on all sides. A wooden board engraved 'Carnival Resto-Bar' at its top. I got down from the scooter and adjusted the heavy rucksack on my shoulder. Punit locked the scooter.

"Are you fine?" Punit asked as he noticed my discomfort.

"This rucksack is too heavy. How does a delicate girl carry it on her shoulders for so long?" I shifted the rucksack from my shoulder to my hand.

The resto-bar was divided into small blocks, all cubical in shape. There was a door to each cube. We entered a cube inside the Carnival. There were two rectangular mats on the floor. In the center was a low table. We sat facing each other on both sides of the table.

"Open and have a look," Punit said as he pushed the rucksack in my hand.

"Is that allowed?" I questioned keeping the rucksack on the table.

"No one is ever going to find out. Even if they reach here, it will take them time to find out which cube we are occupying."

I unzipped Laila's rucksack that she had entrusted to me. It had two black colored fishnet nylon leggings. For a while I imagined Laila wearing those. I could not stop the smile that appeared on my lips. One by one, I started taking other items out of her rucksack. Hundreds of things in all sizes, shapes and colors came out – lipsticks in golden and silver colors, lip balms, perfumes, creams, bindis, earrings, pens, mirrors, wet tissues and other stuff that a girl couldn't live without.

"These are all small things. How is this rucksack so heavy?" I said checking my face in the hand mirror that I had just pulled out from her rucksack. I looked good.

Punit said, "Check the other compartments of the rucksack."

What we saw next was unimaginable. The rucksack had sandals with the highest heels that we had ever seen in our life. Walking in them couldn't be thought of. Standing with those heels on the floor seemed like a tough job. I respect girls for a whole lot of things, and these heels made me respect the owner all the more.

"And that, my friend, is the reason for its heaviness," Punit smiled.

My phone rang. It was Laila.

"Where are you?" she inquired. "We are waiting outside."

"I am sending Punit out," I said and disconnected the call.

Punit went out of the cube to bring them. I kept everything back in the rucksack, zipped each and every part of the rucksack and threw it to a corner of the mat. Everything was perfect when the girls entered the cube.

"I hope we didn't keep you waiting for long," Laila said entering the cube.

"No. We arrived just now," I replied.

"And we had an informative time waiting for you." Punit smiled looking at me.

The girls smiled. Soniya ordered a flavoured hookah for herself. Shreya lit a cigarette and moved around the cigarette box, offering me one.

"Sorry. I don't smoke," I refused.

"I will have one," Punit smiled as he pulled out a cigarette from her box.

Punit almost leaned over Soniya to light his cigarette. A burst of smoke filled the cube. Punit lit another cigarette, creating small circles in the air. We played truth and dare for some time when I saw Laila mumbling something in Soniya's ear.

"Go ahead. Why are you asking me?" Soniya inquired.

"What does she want?" Punit asked.

"She wants to spend some time with Viraj. Can we allow them some privacy?"

"Yes, sure." Punit nodded. I was sure he wanted privacy with the other three girls more.

Nobody asked for my opinion.

"Go man!" Punit smiled as Laila stood up.

I followed her to another cube. We sat facing each other in the new cube. She looked straight into my eyes.

"Are you always like this?" she asked me.

"You mean, I…"

"You are quite shy," she interrupted me.

"Actually, I am not used to meeting so many young and beautiful girls," I spoke gently.

"How are you feeling now?" Her tone had undergone a change as she came a little closer. She sounded seductive.

"It's always good to meet friends," I replied politely.

"I like you."

"What's wrong?" I was surprised.

"I said, I like you," she repeated her words.

"All of a sudden? I mean…"

"It has been more than a month now. We know each other and it was gradual, not a sudden process," she explained.

"I like you too."

"You didn't understand me."

"What do you mean?"

"I like you dude," she was sounding different.

"Me too. That's why we are talking to each other, right?"

"Are you stupid?" she asked incredulously.

"Definitely not."

"Why are you acting as if you don't understand?"

"We both like each other. That's why we are talking to each other. What's not to understand in this?"

"Stupid, I..." she stopped for a moment. "I love you."

I was surprised. I opened my mouth to say something. Laila was faster. She put a finger on my lips, stopping them. She shook her head slowly, asking me not to say anything.

She turned her face towards me. Slowly she closed the distance, bringing her lips near mine. The heartbeats had gone rapid when our lips met. She pressed closer, the kiss grew more intimate. Her actions were potent; they hypnotized me. Her tongue twirled over my lips and she started licking it. I pushed her away, roughly.

"Laila! I can't do this," I said.

She seemed shocked. Slowly as the breaths slowed, the expression on her face turned unpleasant. She touched her lower lips to check her lipstick.

"I am really sorry."

She stared at my face, expressionless.

"I mean you are really gorgeous and really cool. And... And, I am sure every single guy in this universe would cherish you as his girlfriend," I paused for few seconds. "Including me, I just can't, though. I am in love with someone else." I took a deep breath.

I don't know why I said those last few words. Maybe a part of my heart was unable to deny my feelings for Nimisha. God knew I had done everything in my power to forget them.

There was silence in the cube. It could have been hours or just a couple of minutes might have passed. Laila smiled slowly.

"I hope this love of yours goes on, like you say," she said.

"Seriously, I hope that too."

I leaned forward and kissed her on her left cheek. She smiled. "Bye," I said.

I went to Punit and asked him if we could leave. He was unwilling, as he was enjoying the company of the three girls.

"I just remembered I have some urgent work," I said to the girls, waving my hand.

Politics Begins at College

Years had passed since I came to Pune as a student of engineering. By now, life had taught me many lessons. Failure in love, in academics, failure to be a responsible citizen, which had led me to the police station. Failure was something I had accepted in my life, but there was still hope. A desire to somehow make a difference. Every day I went to college with a hope that it would be a new day. Waiting for that day, months had passed. Days changed and so did the news around.

Currently the buzz was 'Vagishyam', the tech fest of our college. Working for the fest meant exposure at all levels to the knowledge of marketing, interacting with different people, thinking independently, human resource management, event management and so on. It was an advantageous tutorial in business. It made one learn, helped personality development and the biggest advantage, free attendance for the semester. That was the reason everyone enjoyed working for it.

I was attending classes, but even I wished to reap benefits of the same. Unfortunately, I was told that it was too late to get involved with the events. I spoke to many of my friends who were holding crucial positions in the Vagishyam team, but everyone expressed inability to help me get in. I had my last hopes pinned on Akshay, my classmate; he was the joint secretary for the big tech fest.

"I want a role in Vagishyam." I was with Akshay in the hall, where he was busy instructing some juniors.

"Okay," he replied without looking at me.

"I have asked many in charge, but they all said I was late. The recruitments for various events are almost done."

"They have no idea, but there will be recruitments for the positions of different event heads in a couple of days," he said as he walked towards one corner of the hall.

"Someone said it will be difficult to get a place there, with so many people coming for interviews. There are just a few positions available."

"Don't worry. I will be there."

"Should I ask Ranjeet too for..." I was stopped by his raised palm.

"You told me, right? It's done. Forget about it."

"Thanks a lot buddy."

"Don't mention it. See you at the interview. Bye." He got back to his work of monitoring volunteers.

I walked out of the hall. I was slightly convinced with Akshay's words, although the future was still hazy.

The notice board had a list of the labs and details of the interviews for the positions of various event heads. We had to choose the events related to our department and the one which interested us.

I made up my mind to go for the interview of Innovation, the B.E. project exhibition for the final year students. "*It will not only give me exposure to the different issues of the event, but I will also have an idea about how the project is to be done in my final year.*"

I greeted Vishwaas and Akshay after entering the interview lab. It felt good to see a friend sitting on the other end of the interview table.

"Good afternoon Viraj," Akshay said.

"So, you are here for the position of event head of Innovation?" Vishwaas inquired.

"Yes, I am," I nodded.

"Tell me. What do you know about the event?" Vishwaas questioned.

"It will be a project exhibition event for final year engineering students from IT and Computers," I explained the little that I knew.

"Were you part of Innovation or any other event team in Vagishyam last year? Maybe, as a volunteer?" he continued.

"Not for Vagishyam. I was in the organizing team of Prastuti, the intra VCOE paper presentation event last year," I said with pride.

"So you have the knowhow to conduct an event," he said as he adjusted himself on the chair.

"Yes. I am good at it."

"Do you need to ask anything, Akshay?" Vishwaas turned to look at Akshay.

"One last question. If you are not selected for Innovation, would you consider any other event? If yes, which one?" Akshay asked a question that I was not sure of.

I thought for a moment and replied, "No."

"Thank you," Akshay finished.

I left them. It was time to give an opportunity to the next interviewee. I stood at a distance and watched. Vikram was next.

"Hello Vikram! How are you?" Akshay questioned.

"I am good, and you?"

"Good. Ready for the interview?"

"Yes."

"What does your father do, Vikram?" Vishwaas asked.

"He is a doctor."

I listened to his answer, shocked. Everyone knew that Vikram's father was in police. When did he change his profession? Thinking was bound to create confusion. It was in my best interest that I got out of there. I got out of the lab. Abhay enquired about the interview. I narrated my experience.

"They didn't ask you much," Abhay said.

I shrugged.

"Maybe you will get selected. Not many from Computers Department are vying for this position."

"I can't say." I couldn't speak about my discussion with Akshay, prior to the interview. "I will leave."

Abhay went inside the interview lab, while I walked towards my classroom.

"Didn't you see the notice board? The names of event heads for all the events have been put up," Punit looked at me questioningly.

"No, I didn't. Really? Are they out?" I asked surprised.

"They are talking about it. Go, have a look," he added and went back to his desk.

I rushed towards Lab 6 to see the results. A long list of event heads for every event was there. I started looking for my name. Most of my friends' names had made to the list. Shikha, Aastha, Manjeet, Abhishek, everyone was an event head. "Oh… Here it is," I said to myself as I noticed the list of event heads for Innovation. It mentioned names from each of the Department.

Innovation

Event Head	Department
1. Muthu Ramaswamy	Computers
2. Sanjay Kulkarni	Computers
3. Chandra Shekhar	I.T.
4. Abhay Sinha	I.T.

I knew that none from the Computers Department had cared to appear for the interview for the position. Their names were proudly displayed on the notice board now! I left the place, hurt. I sauntered to the lab where my practical class was underway. Muthu was coming from the opposite direction.

"Hi Muthu," I greeted him.

"Hi Viraj," he smiled.

"Congrats! You are event head of Innovation," I extended my hand to shake.

He held my palm tightly. "Thank you."

He knew that I wanted that position. He was of course more capable than me for conducting an event like Innovation. However, it was not a question of capability. I questioned the process. *How did a person who didn't follow the procedure get selected for that position?* I knew all these questions were useless after the list was out.

I met Akshay later. He was sitting with some juniors on the stairs. His eyes did not meet mine.

"I have to talk to you."

"Tell me."

"Not here. I want some privacy."

"Everyone here is part of Vagishyam. It's fine."

I waited for a moment. He didn't budge.

"Dog, cat, sheep, goat, pig, everyone constitutes this list of event heads except me," I yelled.

"I can explain."

"You have an explanation?" I was really annoyed.

"Yes, I have."

"For those who did not appear in the interview?"

He didn't say anything. The juniors looked at me with surprise. I stomped away. I made up my mind. I was not going to work in any of the events. Vagishyam was surely not my cup of tea anymore.

A week later

"Don't take me wrong. Just give me two minutes and I will let you know the whole story," Muthu stood from his chair.

"I am listening." I got comfortable on his bed. He stared at me.

"Last year, I was a volunteer in Innovation. I know many seniors and event heads. I wanted to work for an event in Vagishyam too. On the day before your interview, while I was returning from college, I met Pradeep and Amar bhaiya." They were our seniors. "Amar bhaiya was event head for Innovation last year. They asked me about my contribution to Vagishyam this year. I told them that I could not contribute to any, as I was not shortlisted. They asked for my choice. That's how my name appeared on the list."

"Why do you think you need to explain?" I asked him.

"I know that you too wanted the same position."

"I did. But I am not interested anymore."

"I want you to work with me for Innovation," Muthu offered.

"Sorry, I can't," I expressed my helplessness.

"Why so?"

"You know the position for which I went for the interview. If I work now, I will be working as a volunteer."

"Does a position matter so much to you? You will be learning the same skills in the event that you wanted to."

"Still, it does matter to me." I was not going to accept his charity. I knew he was covering up for his guilt.

"I will see to it that you are given the same respect and honour by other volunteers that an event head gets. What do you say now?"

"I need some time to think."

"How much?"

"I don't know. I will let you know of my decision."

"We have a meeting with all the volunteers and those in charge for the event on Monday morning. I will appreciate if you let me know your decision before that."

"I will try," I said as I left.

Innovation

I was the first one to reach the joint entrance of Lab 3 and Lab 4. No volunteers had arrived by that time. Rishabh was the next to join.

"Hi, how are you?"

"I am good. For Innovation?"

"Yes. Muthu bhaiya asked me to be part of the team and come for the meeting."

"Where is he?"

"Here he comes," Rishabh pointed at Muthu who had reached the corridor.

"Good to see you here, Viraj," Muthu said.

"Thanks for the opportunity."

He smiled. When he smiles it feels like one has found a piece of diamond in a coal mine.

We shifted a few chairs to a corner of the lab and formed a closed circle.

"We need to shortlist the B.E. projects for the exhibition," Muthu commenced the meeting, providing me with the login details.

"How many do we need to shortlist?"

"Everyone who participates from our college must be given a chance, while we can select the ones from other colleges," he explained. "We need to keep in mind the space restrictions, and accordingly the numbers that can be comfortably accommodated."

The faculty members allocated as the event in-charges for Innovation joined us in the lab. We moved to form a bigger group. The faculty members sat at the table while the volunteers sat around.

"How is everything going?" One of the faculty members asked.

"They are hard-working students. We need not worry much for our event," Prof Suman expressed confidence.

Checking mails, poster designing and other duties were assigned. I was entrusted with the selection of projects from the submitted abstracts.

Muthu came to my flat that night. We logged in to the college mail to check abstracts of different participants. There were interested participants from colleges all over India. Colleges like IIT Madras, SASTRA and certain others were also participating in the event.

"I am filled up to my neck. It was a heavy dinner. Need to spread out some of that food," Muthu said lying on my bed and resting his head on the pillow. "Read the abstracts one by one. I will listen, and then we will shortlist candidates whose abstracts are good."

I started with the process. When I was tired, Muthu took my place on the chair and I took his place on the bed, listening to the abstracts. By 1 a.m., we had shortlisted candidates with projects that seemed interesting to us. Too lazy to go to his place, Muthu slept at my place that night.

The next task in my line of duty was to make a list of participants who had paid for the event, but had not sent their abstract yet. I had to call them to remind about the last date of submission.

Everything was moving smoothly. Muthu had chosen his team well.

It was time to take a decision about the judges for the event and send them invites. The list contained three types of should-be-judges. The first one was senior teachers from other colleges, second was the faculties from Vagishyam College of Engineering for Women, the shortest list of all and the third and the most important were the people from the industries. They were busier compared to the faculty members. We had to take care of a few things before they came to judge the projects, most important being the days on which they were available. We had to maintain a check of all the available slots.

"We need to send mails to every participant tonight. The mail must contain the list of the documents they need to bring with them," Muthu said as I kept my phone on the table after a long conversation with one of the judges.

"Do they have to bring anything other than their project?" I enquired for details.

"They have to bring their CPUs along with them. The college CPUs are low configuration. The projects of the participants might require higher configured CPUs," Muthu explained to me.

I sent a mail to every participant who was shortlisted for the event.

The labs were crowded with a large number of computers. Three days before the event, we were allocated the required labs. No practical was to be conducted in these labs until the event was over.

"We need to shift the PCs to Prof Choksey's cabin," Chandra Shekhar ordered after noting the current situation of the lab.

I nodded, moving to make an itemized list. Other event heads followed suit.

After moving the computers, we discovered the dust underneath. We had asked the peons several times to clean the tables. None of them had cared to answer the call.

Prof Choksey came to see our work in progress. He saw the condition. Chandra Shekhar informed him that none of the peons had come to the lab, even after repeated instructions. Professor went out of the lab. We relaxed believing Prof Choksey would be able to get the peons. We stared incredulously when Prof Choksey entered the hall with a broom in his hand and started cleaning the desks.

Prof Choksey was to be the HOD of IT Department next year. *If he could clean the desks with a broom, why not us?* Volunteers and event heads looked at each other. I took a step towards our professor and my hands reached out for the broom. The professor looked at me. As my grip on the broom strengthened, the professor let go and occupied a clean corner of the room.

We learnt something that day which was not written in any engineering book. No work in this world should be looked down upon. One should not feel bad if he has to do a small job.

It took us almost two hours to clean the labs. The next job was to paste charts on every lab's walls. The labs were successfully converted into exhibition rooms by the end of the day.

Muthu and I had shortlisted thirty projects. We chose projects in groups of seven or eight, and pasted a sheet with the names of participants and title of every project that needed to be exhibited in a particular lab.

Our faculty in-charge visited us in the evening to check the preparations, critically. She couldn't find any fault.

"Everything looks perfect." Prof Gogate was all appreciation for our labour.

"Thank you, ma'am," Muthu nodded.

"These are the points on which judges will have to evaluate different projects and award marks accordingly." She passed few sheets with long tables.

"Did you all decide the roles that you will be playing during the next three days?"

We discussed the entire plan with the teachers. Event heads were divided into different groups. Sanjay was given charge of the food department. His work was to arrange snacks for judges as they arrived. Two students were asked to stay with the judges. Every judge was given the list of project details and they had to choose four projects they were interested in evaluating. Every judge had to decide on the basis of different criteria.

I was arguing with the guard who was not allowing me to enter college. He was asking me to go to the auditorium to listen to the Vagishyam inaugural speech by our respected principal. Every student who came after me was forced to go. The few who came earlier had managed to escape. I chose not to go there meekly. I stood there trying to convince him.

"I have my event. Let me go in," I requested.

"No. Sir ordered us to send everyone to the auditorium," he said moving his stick to say no.

I called up Muthu who was already present in the lab. After a few minutes, Sanjay came to the entrance. He said something to the guard in Marathi, after which the guard allowed me to enter.

"You should have come earlier," Sanjay said as we took the stairs to the labs on the upper floor.

"I was arranging judges' sheets till late last night."

Everything seemed to be in place. We were ready to welcome our participants. We made a small reception between the entrance of the two labs. The participants arrived with their CPUs. We allowed them to enter labs after assigning unique identification numbers.

"How can we allow you if your name is not there in this list?" I asked a participant, who was standing near the reception with his CPU.

"I sent my abstract to Innovation's mail ID," he argued without any proof.

"Did you receive a confirmation mail to come for the event?" I asked him.

"But I am from this college."

"What's the problem Viraj?" Muthu interrupted the senior and my conversation.

"This gentleman's name is not there in the list. Nor did we call him for the event. Still he wants to exhibit his project," I informed.

"Come here for a minute," Muthu pushed me to a corner.

"Wait a minute, sir," I excused myself from the senior.

"Do they belong to our college?" Muthu asked.

"Yes, they do, but we haven't received an abstract from their end. How could we shortlist them?"

"We can't send back a participant from our own college. That's the rule."

"This may create confusion. We won't have any details of this project anywhere in our list or the list the judges would be having," I said.

"I will look over it. You just adjust them somewhere," Muthu said moving upstairs.

I looked for a vacant space in the appointed labs. Two of the project groups had not arrived. I adjusted the new group in one of the spaces.

Almost every participant had taken their place. We instructed them to be ready with their projects. At around noon, our judges arrived. Sanjay took them for refreshments first. Kavika and I instructed them to different labs depending on the projects they chose.

Most of the volunteers were found missing from their assigned labs as they chose to visit other events. Few hands including mine were the only available. At four in the evening, when I was dying with hunger, Raksha came with few food coupons that we could use. Everyone chose the opportunity to do as they wished. By the time we returned, lack of monitoring had led to chaos. Prof Gogate was furious with the turn the event had taken. She instructed each and every event head and volunteer to stay in the labs after the event.

"What is the explanation for what happened today?" she almost shouted at me.

"I did my duty well. There was no delay in any judge's chance to evaluate projects," I tried to clarify my role.

"It's not about you. We are conducting a team event. If an event is a failure, every one of us is responsible." Her eyes rained sparks on everyone in the lab.

I didn't have an answer.

"The judges' evaluation sheets will be with volunteers tomorrow. There will be fewer movements for sheets," she instructed.

"Sorry ma'am. I don't think it will be good to give important documents in the hands of second year students," I opposed.

"What do you expect then? I don't want my event to be a failure," she explained.

"Just instruct them to be in the labs they are assigned. I will take care of the rest."

"I leave it to you then."

She told off the volunteers for another five minutes before declaring it the end of the day. The next day was surely to be tougher.

Everything looked better the next day. That day, none of the volunteers left their places. In the afternoon, Prof Choudhary visited the labs to inspect our event. He left, praising Muthu for good management.

A new problem was heard soon. The evaluation sheet of Naini, a sought after girl from final year engineering, had been tampered with.

I was walking with one of the judges after he listened to a project with great interest. Chandra Shekhar approached the judge, instructing him in Marathi, while he gave marks in the evaluation sheet in his hand. I could not get anything from their conversation, except that the judge was giving exactly the same marks as instructed by him. I didn't say a word to the judge or Chandra Shekhar. I guided the judge till the exit door, then went to look for Muthu.

"Hey, I need to talk to you," I said. Muthu was almost running towards one of the labs.

"I am busy right now. Later."

"Stop. It's very urgent," I almost shouted.

He stopped. "What is it?"

"Did Chandra Shekhar call Amit?"

Amit was the judge who had left after evaluating a few projects just then.

"Yes, he is his relative working in TCS. What's the problem?"

"Take all evaluation sheets under your control."

"What's the matter?" Lines breaking his smeared tilak indicated that he was worried.

I narrated the incident to Muthu. It took him a few minutes to accept what he had heard. He agreed with me, and then went upstairs. I looked at him puzzled. At the end of the day, Muthu sat in a cabin with Prof Suman and all the evaluation sheets. No faculty in-charge or event head was allowed there.

Muthu joined me near the exit after almost an hour.

"Is everything okay?"

"Yes. It's fine. There had been some overwriting in Naini's evaluation sheet," he said.

"Okay. Are the results ready?"

"Almost."

"You did a good job," I said.

"As long as you are there. Thank you," he said with a smile.

"Don't be mad. Let's go to Ghazal Night. Your sister-in-law is going to sing today," I joked as Nimisha was going to perform a song for the crowd that evening.

He laughed out loudly. We sauntered towards the stage where the Ghazal Night was to begin soon.

Muthu and I reached the lab by 8:30 the next morning. We were all dressed in kurtas and jeans, the uniform decided for the occasion. We looked different in the crowd of students.

We arranged the lab to resemble a prize distribution hall in an hour.

"Something is still missing," Muthu said looking at the table where judges were to sit.

"What's missing now?" I enquired.

"Haven't you noticed, in every big prize ceremony, they have water on the table in front of the judges?"

"Do you think college will pay for these extravagances?" I asked.

"We are not going to buy bottles."

"Then?" I was puzzled.

"There are numerous bottles used in the last two days. Collect all the undamaged ones. Let us get water from the tap," he smiled as he spoke those words.

An engineering student's tenure in college is wasted if they do not learn the most important lesson. The lesson in 'jugaad'.

At 10:30 a.m., teachers sat on their chairs while the participants faced them. Muthu wanted me to host the event. After shouting for the past two days, my voice resembled that of a damaged flute. It could only be used to terrify little kids if they refused to empty their milk bottles. Rishabh joined Kavika in anchoring the prize distribution ceremony.

It started with facilitating the faculty members with bouquets. The results were announced and prizes were distributed among participants. The faculty members left after the prize distribution, while the event heads and volunteers stayed back for taking pictures. Few participants later came to us and asked to see the marks they had obtained. We showed them the evaluation sheets.

"Bhaiya, come outside. There is some problem," a disturbed Rishabh disturbed me.

As soon as I stepped out I saw Naini, Abhijit and Rutuja shouting at the volunteers. The three were involved in the same project.

"What do you think of yourselves?" Abhijit grumbled.

"What happened, sir?" I asked Abhijit.

"You have been bribed for the event. You thought we wouldn't catch you?" He was screaming at the top of his voice.

"What are you talking about?"

"I went to see the result. Your organizers are not willing to show it."

"Where is Muthu?" I asked Rishabh.

"At Bull's Station," Abhijit shouted at me for the third time.

"Please don't talk so loudly and create a scene," I requested him politely, although I felt like hitting him hard.

You can't hit a senior, no matter how rude they are. It's absolutely impossible when you are standing opposite to your principal's cabin.

"What do you want from us?" I asked.

"The prize distribution is over. You can't do shit now," Abhijit seethed. "But being a junior, Muthu should not have insulted us. He should apologize to us. We will stand here until he does so."

"Just give me two minutes." I went upstairs to look for Muthu.

He was busy enjoying a game on one of the PCs.

"Don't you know what's going on downstairs?"

"Yeah, I know." He said in a tired voice.

"So? Can't you show them their evaluation sheets?"

"I did that already. But they are not happy seeing them just once. I refused the third time they came." He looked at me.

"They are creating a scene outside the principal's cabin."

"Viraj, so far you have handled everything related to the event most efficiently. I know you will be the best man to handle them. Please."

I went downstairs.

"Sir, he is not there. I think he left for his hostel. He is not picking up his phone either. I have your number. I will give you a call," I said to console Abhijit.

"Don't you try to be as smart as Muthu," Naini's pitch rose this time.

"I am not trying to," I lowered my voice.

Other volunteers tried to calm them, but they stayed adamant.

"Muthu is not aware, but the Concepts group was created in my room. I will ruin his remaining life in this college," Abhijit roared.

The Concepts group was a group of techies from different departments who were involved in creating different events all round the year. Muthu was one of the active members of that group.

"Enough is enough," I finally lost my temper. "My mother used to tell me when I was a kid – *Hathi chale bazaar, kutte bhaunke hazaar.* That when a person who does not exhibit much importance shouts at you, ignore them. Leave these fuckers over here. Let us go," I instructed my volunteers.

"You will have to pay for this," Abhijit said swaying his fingers at me. His face had turned red.

"I am not afraid to pay for any of my deeds." I left with my volunteers.

We came back to our lab. We could see them standing there for a while, irritated, frustrated and insulted by us. They left after they could not find anyone who would listen to them. I went to Muthu and we had lunch together. I rushed to my flat and packed my luggage to leave for my hometown.

A few moments before the train's departure, I texted Muthu.

'Thanks a lot for giving me an opportunity when nobody cared. i know i had been rude and not perfect on many occasions. still the last six days will always be memorable to me. good bye.'

This event had done me good. It had given me the confidence that I had forgotten. As the train left the station, my mobile showed the delivery report for the message.

No Submissions

Chandra Shekhar rushed to me while I was studying in the reading hall. The semester exams were approaching.

"Prof Sule is looking for Muthu and you. Where is Muthu?" he huffed.

"I don't know. What's the matter?"

"I am not aware of that exactly. But Prof Sule was tensed," he added, sitting on the chair beside me.

I called Muthu.

"I got a call from Sanjay too that she is looking for me," Muthu said.

"Let's get to the college then," I said and disconnected the phone.

Within fifteen minutes, I don't remember how many of our friends came and repeated, "Prof Sule is looking for Muthu and you."

I was frightened, but not frightened out of my wits. I started recalling all the things that could have annoyed her. However, I was unable to find even one reason. Muthu had no idea either. We rushed towards her cabin where she was busy working on her computer.

"What have you guys done?" Prof Sule asked us as soon as we entered her cabin.

"Sorry ma'am. We have no idea what you are talking about," Muthu replied equally surprised.

"Prof Baitha has asked me to stop submissions of your journals."

Not in a hundred years we could have guessed this development. Puzzled, we went mute. Prof Baitha was a senior faculty member from the IT Department. Stopping submissions meant we wouldn't be allowed to appear in any of our practical or orals. It was equivalent to three to four backlogs in the semester. I stood quietly. Nothing went in my ears after her last word. Future flashed in front of my eyes. *Will I be able to complete my degree in just four years? Should I apologize for anything and everything I did? I am not aware of the reason for this punishment. Could I rewind my engineering life to start all over again?*

"What have you two done? Tell me," she demanded again.

"We are not aware of what we have done, ma'am. We haven't ever spoken to Prof Baitha," Muthu cried. I still stood silent, trying to regain my senses.

"Go and find out. What should I do at this moment, when I am instructed by a senior professor?" She showed her helplessness.

Since Prof Baitha was from the IT Department, we thought our friends from that department may have some knowledge of the issue. We came to know the whole matter from Raksha.

Prof Baitha was Naini and the group's project guide for their final year project. After she lost in Innovation last month, she had been acting weird. She did not visit her project guide and let him know through her friends that she was depressed with the faulty result during the fest. She said she needed time to recover from the situation. I never understood why a teacher had taken her so seriously. Prof Baitha had chosen a penalty that could ruin us.

We reached Prof Sule's cabin after finding the facts. We told her everything.

"Go and listen to whatever Professor Baitha says," she said. "And listen! Don't argue with him if he says something rude. Let me know. Go now."

She picked up her phone to make a call to someone. She waved her hand, asking us to leave. Muthu and I discussed everything that we were to say in Prof Baitha's cabin before we entered.

We stood outside his cabin. He saw us. A smile appeared on his face, a sign of victory. We did not respond. He called us after a few minutes.

"Good morning sir," we chorused.

"I don't think your morning can be worse than this. Tell me, what can I do for you?" He was mocking us rudely.

"Professor Sule asked us to meet you," Muthu said.

"Who is Muthu and who is Viraj?"

"I am Viraj and he is Muthu," I pointed at Muthu.

"So, you both are the guys who think they can do anything in this college?"

We did not respond.

"I had a talk with your HOD regarding this matter. You should meet him," he made the floor slip from under my feet in seconds.

"Yes sir," Muthu said.

"You are the one who roams with that girl every day in the college? You will face worse consequences if I see you again with that girl," Prof Baitha looked at Muthu.

I believe he had seen Muthu with Jaswinder. Jaswinder Kaur, a Punjabi kudi was our classmate and Muthu's first day crush in college.

"You can leave now."

We left his cabin and straight away entered Prof Sule's. In a few minutes, we were standing outside the HOD's cabin. I felt limp as I entered his cabin. Prof Suman stood outside his cabin to support us. It was really necessary at that moment.

"Tell me the complete story," the HOD demanded.

"Sir, we didn't do anything. We are the organizers of Innovation. What is our mistake if a participant or a group does not win in an event?" Muthu questioned.

"I can understand that. I have been part of various events. I trust my volunteers. Do you have phone numbers of any participants who complained to Baitha?" His supportive words made me feel better.

"I am not sure. I believe Abhay may have Abhijit's number," I replied.

"Get me his number," he ordered.

Muthu stayed in the cabin while I walked out to arrange for his number. I called Abhay and asked for Abhijit's number. He took a minute to forward it to me. I passed the number to our HOD after writing it on a small piece of paper. He placed the slip under his pad and started dialling the number. After a minute, he said to us, "He is not picking up my call. Don't worry. I will talk to him. You both can leave now."

We were about to leave when he asked, "How many of you were event heads of Innovation?"

"Four," Muthu replied.

"Next time you come, come along with all event heads."

We walked out and called every other event head in college. A few days ago, Abhay was depressed as he had been unable to see the final evaluation sheets. He felt very happy and relieved now. The peon called us to the HOD's cabin a little later. All event heads and I followed Muthu to the HOD's cabin. The peon stopped me at the entrance, "Sir is calling only the event heads."

I felt relieved. *Who the hell wants to visit his cabin thrice in a single day?* But within five minutes, I was called in.

"What did the guys tell you after the event?" the HOD asked. "Regarding Concepts, I mean."

"Abhijit said that Concepts was created in his room. He will ruin Muthu's remaining life in college..." I repeated Abhijit's words after the prize distribution ceremony.

"What the hell does he think of himself? Stopping my volunteers' submissions. He has forgotten his limits," HOD sir said angrily as he waved to the peon to come inside.

"I called the guy again, but he is not answering his phone. Let me talk to the guy once and..."

I interrupted my HOD, "He is sitting in the lab opposite Professor Baitha's cabin. If you want, I can call him."

"Thank you, folks. You can leave now. Only Muthu and Viraj need to stay here," he ordered the other event heads.

Everyone else left the room. Sanjay signalled me with his eyes to maintain my calm and that everything would be fine.

"You don't call them. Just take him along with you and show him the boy," HOD sir said pointing towards his peon. "He will call them. Meet me after half an hour."

We went out with his peon towards the lab where Abhijit and Rutuja were in a discussion. I stood outside the lab and pointed at Abhijit and Rutuja. The peon instructed us to leave.

We hid behind the window of the lab. We saw Abhijit and Rutuja entering the HOD's cabin. They were in there for a long time. The peon did not allow anyone to enter the cabin. After almost twenty minutes, both of them came out. I could see a ninety degree fall on their faces while they were climbing the stairs. Muthu and I went into the cabin after ten minutes.

"I hope they won't be a problem anymore. They are here only for a few more months. Don't get too worried," the HOD continued.

"It will be very kind of you if you can talk to Professor Baitha. He is a senior faculty member and may take some of our subjects in the coming semesters," Muthu requested.

"He won't be a problem. Don't worry a..."

"Sir, if you would just speak to him once, we could relax," Muthu insisted.

HOD nodded and instructed his peon to call Prof Baitha. "You two stay in the lab, I will be calling you after I speak with him."

We both came out and stood behind the window again. Prof Baitha entered HOD sir's cabin with a smile on his face. He was not aware of what had taken place since we met him this morning. When he came out of the cabin, we could see his face was red. I think we had won the battle. The HOD's peon called us after a minute. We went in for the fifth time in a single day.

"Everything is taken care of."

"Thank you sir," Muthu said.

"Best of luck for your practicals and submissions." He smiled.

"Thanks for your cooperation," I said as we left his cabin.

Bad Sector

The backlogs of my theory papers had been fluctuating. It changed from one to three from first to second semester and kept fluctuating between two to three after that. However, I managed to clear all my orals and practical exams till semester five.

Programming in C or C++ had become my passion since the second year. My website, where I used to upload my practical assignments, was very popular among students. Guys and girls I didn't even know were regular visitors to my website and had bookmarked my site for further use.

"Don't give your programs to anyone else," my professors told me most of the time as I was among the first few to get my assignments checked in class.

However, there is always an exception to what each and everyone can do. The exception for me was CO – Computer Organization. It was different from other programming languages because the programs had to be done on assembly language. Every engineering student was scared of the language. Past year records showed maximum number of failures in its practical exam.

To overcome the difficulty in practical, many including Muthu and I had joined CO tuitions at Swargate. It was difficult to even copy programs from notebooks to computers and make them work. Every time you ran it, it showed a different result.

The most difficult thing about this practical was that one of the invigilators in the practical in most of the cases was Prof Choksey, a knowledgeable Computer Engineer and a very strict man.

The final day came. Many among us had by-hearted programs line by line. A few like me had tried to grasp the program as much as possible.

It was heard earlier that programs in practical exam would come from the journal we had prepared throughout the semester. However, in the final practicals, few programs were unforeseen. It didn't matter much to the students because almost all of us knew which programs in our journals were working and showed the output.

We were also aware about the manipulation we did in output in a notepad and got it checked by the concerned faculty. Seeing the case of the previous day's practical exams for the same subject, many like Punit came with a pen drive. Cowards like me were trying to have their last look at the programs in their journals.

"C'mon guys, keep your journal with you. Switch off all mobile phones you have in your pockets and keep them in your bags. Enter the hall one by one," Prof Choksey shouted as the clock hit 1:30 p.m.

We prayed to almighty to save us from Prof Choksey and entered the hall. Prof Saumya sat on the first bench of the hall with a stack of blank sheets and the attendance sheet with her.

Everyone walked to her, signed the attendance sheet in front of their exam sheet number and picked a blank sheet from the bundle. In every sheet, there was a note that mentioned the program one had to do.

Vikram went with his sheet. I signed in the attendance sheet and faced Prof Saumya. She shifted the papers towards me and said, "Choose one among them."

I closed my eyes and randomly selected one. When I opened my eyes as well as the blank paper, I was blown away. It was the only program in the journal that was not running. I had tried to run it several times but had never succeeded.

I hurriedly moved the sheet back in the bundle, between the two sheets and slowly spoke to Prof Saumya, "This is the only program I didn't do."

She looked to her right. She looked to her left and ordered me quickly, "Pick up another one fast."

I picked another one. It read: *Counting the number of bad sectors in a floppy disk.*

"Did you do this?" She looked at me half hopeful, half scared.

"Yes ma'am. I did," I answered with a smile.

She took my paper, wrote the number that was adjacent to the program and returned my sheet, "Carry on."

"Thank you," I said as I left her desk.

At another desk, I wrote an algorithm and an instruction set that I was going to use in the program. I wrote the necessary details in my answer sheet and passed my answer sheet to Prof Choksey. He verified the algorithm and asked a question about the instruction set that I could answer quite easily. I was assigned a system to write the program. Prof Choksey left after checking the answer sheets of almost all the students.

The external teacher came to ask me a few more questions. I answered almost all of them like a parrot who had mugged the whole book. I didn't wish to fail in my practical exams.

I typed the program in another hour and asked for a floppy disk to check the number of bad sectors in it. I inserted the floppy disk and ran my program. It could not show me number of bad sectors in it. I was a little tense. I took out floppy disk and re-inserted it. I ran the code again. There was no change in the output. I thought for a moment, checked my program, but couldn't find an error.

May be this floppy disk is not working. I should ask for another one, I muttered to myself.

I tried it with another floppy disk and then, with the third one. The expected output still did not appear on the screen. The perspiration ran down from somewhere behind my right ear. The fear of failing in my practical exam was making me restless.

"What happened?" Prof Suman asked, noticing my discomfort.

She was standing right behind me. She could clearly see that a student of her class was in trouble.

I turned back, looked at her and said softly, "My program is not working."

"Oui…" she thought for a moment. "I have a pen drive which has all the programs. Don't worry. I will bring it for you. Act as if you are still typing the program."

Prof Suman was a lovely lady who had completed her engineering a year ago from some college in Madhya Pradesh. She joined our college after her graduation. She gained a lot of respect in her short duration at college. Her Orkut status showed single and her smile was something that any student in our batch was prepared to die for. Right now, to me, she was an angel who was helping me pass my practicals.

I behaved as if I was typing for the next fifteen minutes while she came and kept her pen drive in front of my monitor. She went away quietly. I looked at her, but she was gone.

I swapped her pen drive in my pocket, waited for the invigilator to move to the other corner in the hall and slowly pushed the pen drive into the slot where it was meant to be. I didn't open the pen drive directly, but opened each and every program in the compiler. The blue screen kept me safe. I checked all the thirteen programs in the pen drive but my bad luck was awesomely very good. It was quite queer. It contained all the programs except the one I required. I pulled out the pen drive and went towards Prof Suman.

I placed the pen drive in her right palm and whispered in her ears, "It has all the programs in the journal except the one I need."

She said quite loudly, "What now?" My tension seemed to have transferred to her face.

"Let me think," I whispered.

"If Choksey sir enters the hall, I won't be able to help you by any means," she said.

She had a point. Whatever I had to do, it needed to be done before the demon entered. I thought for a moment and whispered to the professor, "Punit has brought a pen drive."

She understood my intention and asked me to return to my seat. She went to Punit's computer.

"Punit, give me your pen drive," she said.

"Which pen drive? Where?" His voice was trembling.

"C'mon! Viraj told me that you have it. His program is not working," she moved forward her hand towards Punit.

He looked at my face from his place and his facial expression said, *Why the hell did you tell her?*

I looked at him and my facial expression could say, *I need to pass, man.*

"Give it to me," Prof Suman demanded.

"Ma'am, take a round of the hall and come back. I will give it to you."

"Don't delay. If Choksey sir enters the hall, nothing will be possible." Her hand was still out.

"Ma'am, just take a small round."

"Give it to me now," she ordered, frustrated.

Punit put his hand inside his denims. He stopped momentarily but then his hand was looking for something in his underwear. He took out the pen drive, and kept it in her palm. Her mouth fell wide open. She was the only one responsible for this predicament. Punit had been given no option. She walked slowly towards me and kept the pen drive on my outstretched palm.

I easily found the required program. I saved the program with my exam sheet number in the system's disk and put the pen drive in my pocket. Prof Choksey entered a few minutes later.

"Suman, did you check all the programs? You start checking from this side and I will join you in another minute," Prof Choksey pointed towards me.

Prof Suman said to Prof Choksey after a minute, "His program is working well."

I thanked Prof Suman and Prof Choksey and went out of the hall, relieved.

The Unexpected

"How long have you been doing this?" Sahil's tongue snaked towards the ice cream in his hand.

"I made new habits last semester, and now they have become my lifestyle."

"Interesting, huh."

It was two at night. Sahil was discussing my habit of blogging. He had joined me that day to try an ice cream. Richie Rich's business flourished by catering to people like me at this hour.

I kick-started my bike. Astride, I tried to reverse it with a jerk. Maybe the tire hit a pebble with the jerk, because the very next moment, I lay on the uneven pavement while the bike was scraping the road. Sahil rushed to the bike and picked it up. I was still rolling on the ground clutching my aching body.

"Are you okay?"

"I can't stand."

"C'mon dude. You are a tiger. Try to sit up first," he offered his hand for leverage.

I caught his hand tightly, nearly smashing it. Standing took a lot of effort. He gave me the bike keys.

"I don't think I will be able to drive. Could you? Please…" I was in too much pain.

He cautiously accelerated. The bike seemed fine. At least that did not have any damage. I, on the other hand, felt lifeless. My right elbow hurt unbearably. I tried to rest it in a comfortable posture, but nothing helped. We were back at my place. I tried to study to distract myself from the pain, but that was all I could concentrate on. I thought sleep would help, but trying to fall asleep was a waste of time. I just couldn't.

The pain refused to subside even after three hours. I switched on the light. I could not even straighten my hand. It had frozen at a right angle. I tried to wake up Sahil, who was snoring. When he did not respond to my painful cries, I kicked his bed with my left leg.

"Did you push my bed?"

"No, it was an earthquake."

"Is it? That woke you as well?" He rubbed his eyes.

"Can you move your butt out of that bed? I am unable to straighten my hand."

Sahil jumped out of his bed in a jiffy reached for my hand making an acute angle by then, and applied force on it to turn it into a normal one.

"Stop!" I screamed. "It hurts."

"Try to sleep. We will visit a doctor in the morning," Sahil suggested.

"No, I have suffered for the past three hours. I know I can't sleep. We have to go a doctor right now," I decreed.

"It's 5:30 in the morning. Do you think we will find a doctor now?"

"I have heard Bhandari hospital stays open 24 hours."

"Fine," Sahil reached for his clothes.

Thankfully, the hospital was open. The on call doctor pierced my aching hand to administer a painkiller. I was taken for an X-ray.

We got the report in half an hour. It said a ligament had torn. We returned to my home with a plaster extending from my biceps to the palm. Punit opened the door.

"What happened?" He was surprised.

"Ligament torn," Sahil replied.

"How come? You know, we have exams after two days," he looked at me as if I was silly to have done it.

"Few things happen without invitation. I didn't sleep the entire night. I am sleepy." I stretched on my bed.

I couldn't find a comfortable position. The pain was too much. Finally cradling my hand between my stomach and pillow, I fell asleep.

When I woke up, I tried hard to study. My hand could not rest, nor my mind. I passed a rope through the overhead hook. No, I was not attempting suicide. I tied a knot between the two ends, forming a loop. I passed my hand through the loop. It now hung freely. No pain to distract me!

"Tough studying in this state," Punit sympathized.

"With two days for the semester exams to begin, you don't really have a choice," I stated.

"I would have given up. There is always next semester."

"I am trying as much as I can."

"I see your efforts," he smiled.

I studied in that posture for the next two days.

"How can we inform you of an injury before it happens?" Punit argued with an Examination Department staff. We were there to request a writer.

"We can't do anything," the staff replied, bored.

"Do think, sir. The accident happened on Sunday. Yesterday was a holiday. We are informing you in the first opportunity," Punit rationalized.

"Look. We don't have writers waiting for you. The rules clearly explain, that one needs to ask for a writer three days in advance." The man pointed to the rules stuck on the notice board.

"The system is fucked up." Punit was frustrated.

"Let's go Punit. I will manage without a writer," I pulled him away. The staff had taken offence at his cursing.

"At least let me put in a request for later exams," I requested them and did the needful.

"You will be late. Go to your examination hall. I am going into mine. Best of luck," I waved my aching arm.

I tried to support my hand with the desk. I could not write. The invigilator kept the question paper on my desk and smiled. I tried to smile back, but it didn't come. I removed the bandage that ran through my neck. I started with my paper, trying to tackle as much as possible before the hand gave up.

I knew I had fared badly in all the papers. I prayed to god to let me complete my engineering in four years.

I had just two backlogs in my third year. However, I was still awaiting the second year's backlog results. Punit joined me when I went to collect my second year mark-sheet. Prof Suman sat in the lab with the yet unclaimed mark-sheets. She searched but could not find mine.

"Somebody might have taken it," she fiddled with the bundle.

"I didn't ask anyone to collect it."

She found it on the third attempt, "Here it is."

I looked at my Maths marks. I had failed.

"Is everything okay?" she asked.

"I failed," I muttered.

She did not respond. I walked out of the lab. Punit followed me. We walked to our house that we had rented for the last year. Now, it was meant for the second last year! I kept my mark-sheet on the computer table, dropped on the bed and closed my eyes.

I could see a dark future. A jobless degree which would come in long five years. I called up my dad and informed him about my results. He didn't say anything. Back home, I had been a good student, a favourite of teachers, topper of subjects and here I was, with my poorest mark-sheet.

Punit used to go to college in the morning while I performed fluid excreting exercises with my eyes. On a Saturday, they went to Sahil's cousin's place for celebrating his birthday. I chose to stay alone in the flat. Nikhil came to keep me company.

"How much time do you need?" My friends were losing patience.

"I don't have a definite date."

"Let's go out to drink. It will cool your mind."

"You know, for me it is not the solution."

"You can have spicy chicken. How long have you been eating at home? Life can't be lived behind closed doors."

I reluctantly changed into a pair of jeans and a shirt. My clothes weren't ironed. I didn't bother combing my hair.

"Let's go."

We rode along the Pune-Mumbai highway. Soon, we were in a dhaba by the side of the road.

"A spicy chicken butter masala, tandoori roti and a small bottle of Magic Moments, green apple with a bottle of Thums Up for me," Nikhil placed the order.

The waiter had just turned to leave when Nikhil said, "Bring two empty glasses."

"I am not going to drink," I said as the waiter left with his order.

"You will have cold drink na?" he spoke lightly.

"Just a little."

"You can have a little vodka too. It will relieve you from your mental pain."

"I can do without it."

"Come on! *Thoda to le*... have a little."

"Don't force me."

The waiter returned with a chilled bottle of Magic Moments Vodka, a Thums Up and two transparent glasses to serve it. Nikhil instructed him to leave. A beautiful chilled, transparent bottle with a black cap was placed before me. A man's image dancing with several ladies was on the bottle. The label read 'Smooth flavoured vodka – Green Apple.'

Nikhil opened the cap of the bottle. He poured a little in a glass and placed it in front of me. I rudely pushed his hand. The drink splashed.

"I hate it. Wastage of good vodka!" he exclaimed.

"Sorry."

"Finish your glass," he instructed.

I took the glass to my lips, a sip and alas! It was the worst taste that ever hit my mouth. It tasted like a thousand expired medicines.

"Yuck! It's awful. How do you people drink it?" I was still reeling with the shocking taste.

"It's the best taste, man."

I forced the glass to my mouth and emptied it. Nikhil tilted the bottle into my glass.

"No more. Please," I requested.

He stopped, "You know you are a man with no life. That's why people talk behind your back, that's why Nimisha left you, that's why you have..."

At the mention of Nimisha's name, I lost it. I picked up the bottle, put it to my mouth and gulped its content. I could taste the fire of hell, flowing from my throat to my belly. Within a minute, the bottle was empty. My head felt giddy. The pain was sweet now. Nikhil ordered another bottle. I was not in my senses. I don't remember how many tandoori rotis I ate. Did the waiter apply butter on it or not? Was the chicken he brought spicy? Nikhil paid the bill when we were done.

"I want to go to college," I said.

"Now?" Nikhil was surprised.

"Yes, right now."

He rode to college and parked his bike near the entrance.

We walked leisurely. Nikhil chose a seat opposite to a statue near the bank. The famous Maratha warrior sat on his horse proudly, the sword held tightly in his hand.

"Come down, you son of a bitch," I shouted.

It looked at me with its large eyes. I stared at him unmoved.

"What are you staring at? If you have the guts, come down from your horse and wrestle with me." I was not a good wrestler, but the vodka in me had started speaking.

"Have you gone mad? The security guards will hear you," Nikhil shushed me.

"Let them. I will teach a lesson to everyone who is responsible for ruining my life."

"Nobody is. Let's go."

"I don't want to go. I want to fight him. He thinks he can scare me with his horse and sword?"

"We will come tomorrow to fight with him. Battles are suspended after sunset. It's written in the *Gita,*" Nikhil said as he held my hand.

"I don't want to go," I shouted at him.

"Who is there?" Someone shouted from a distance.

"I pray to you man. Please come, I have to get to my bike." He dragged me as if I was a heavy sack. We sat on his bike and he rode towards my flat.

"You know something. You are my brother," I whispered in his ear. Isn't it a universal dialogue when one is drunk with friends?

"Yes, I know." He got down from his bike. He managed to put it on stand while I still sat on it. He dragged me to my room. We sat in my room listening to music. I continued to curse and shout at people who weren't there.

"Should I stay here with you for tonight?" Nikhil turned up the volume of the sound system.

"No, I am okay." I felt strangely relieved.

"Give me a call if you need anything," he said and he picked up his keys from the computer table.

I closed the door and lay on the bed. I cried for an hour, and then my stomach began to ache. I retched. I managed to reach the washroom before a nasty smell filled the space. I cried for a few more minutes before I finally fell off to asleep.

I tried to look for ways to pass time. I had lost interest in anything that I picked up. I spent the entire day alone. Punit and Sahil would come in the evening and force me to go out, but I would not go. I started avoiding everyone who cared for me. If I loved something those days, it was my loneliness.

It was nearly a month since my result, which had finalized that I was to stay in college for an extra year. My dad promised several times that he would come to visit me. Later a phone call would inform me he was occupied with elections at one place or another.

A thought always came to me in my hours of loneliness. I had managed to screw up this birth of mine. I should finish it before it worsened. Maybe the next life would be better. Like a perfect life is supposed to be. Several ways of committing suicide came to my mind. I could hang myself to a fan. But it meant bad memories for Punit and Sahil. They would not be able to continue living in this flat. My landlord would not be able to lease it to anyone. I could have swallowed a dozen sleeping pills. But the medical shop refused to sell it without a prescription. I could have slashed my wrist, but I could not take the pain. I thought of eating rat kill for a moment. The next moment I was sure, I didn't want to die a rat's death. A lot of ideas floated in my mind, but none felt good enough.

One evening when I was alone, I went to the Pune-Mumbai highway. Jain Mandir was a place where we spent a lot of our spare time during the engineering course. It was situated on a small hill above the national highway. I started climbing the road to the temple. I didn't reach the temple. The small hill to my left pulled me to it. I started climbing the hill. It was difficult, the path that I had chosen to climb, but I didn't care to climb the hill the way other people did.

I stood on the cliff. Tiny droplets of water glistened on the green grass that covered the hard black rocks. The city of Pune appeared minuscule. The sprawls looked like ants. The vehicles passing by honked hard, but a distant noise was all I could hear. The sky above was darker than ever. The black clouds appeared as giants, resembling the black pages of my life – ugly and dark. The ground below called out to me. I was sure if I jumped from here, I would have only one destiny. I would end up in *hell*.

I reached the ledge's end. My legs shivered. I knew, one more step and I will be lost forever. But I had no choice. If I lived, I would have to be answerable to the world, to my friends, relatives. If I died, it would be an end to my pathetic life. I was not brave. So if being a coward rid me of all my pains, I was prepared to be one.

The sky thundered. Soon, fat droplets hit my face. I closed my eyes. Stream of water trickled down my ears to reach the hard surface under my feet. I felt cold inside. I was not hurt, neither was I in pain. I just could not feel, could not think. The incidents that had brought me to this day flashed before my eyes. It was the last day of my engineering, and my life.

The memories erupted from every part of my brain. I was lost.

A loud ring on my phone broke my trance. I looked at my phone. 'Papa calling…' I was numb, I couldn't pick it. *What will I say to him? What was I going to do?* I didn't have an answer.

I closed my eyes, took a deep breath and raised my left leg. It hung in the air. I was soon going to feel the gravitational force of earth. My phone started ringing again. My dad was waiting for me. I pulled back my feet to its original position. I took his call.

"Hello! Where are you?" my dad asked.

I didn't have an answer.

"Why were you not picking up my call?" I could feel the tension in his voice.

A drop of tear rolled down my left eye.

"Are you crying? Tell me," he insisted, worried.

I don't know what telepathy our parents have with us. We stay thousands of kilometres away. Still, they can feel our pain. Words are not the only medium of communication.

"I am okay," I lied.

"Are you alone? Not at home?" he asked softly.

"I am okay, Papa," I repeated.

"Go back home. I am booking the next flight to Pune. Don't worry," he assured me.

I broke down. I just wanted a hug from my dad that very moment. I needed him.

"No mark-sheet made in this world tells you about the abilities of a child. If at all, it tells you about a few numbers that will be forgotten, sooner or later. There might be a bunch of great scorers in every class. I don't want you to be one among them. I want you to be a great learner. A mark-sheet is someone else's way of telling you who you are. But always remember Viraj, you're the creator of your own life.

"I have cherished all your success. I love you for them. Don't you remember how happy I was when you topped your class? I love you with all your failures too. Trust me, if my son is with me, I can fight the entire world. Don't feel bad. I am proud of being your father and will always be."

"I am also proud of you, Papa," I cried like a baby.

"Go back home. I will be there tomorrow morning. I promise."

"Yes."

I slipped my phone back into my pocket and climbed down the hill. I could have gone to visit the temple. But I tried to imagine what god would look like. Like my dad, I was sure.

Difference between Me and a 'Maratha'

The day I had received that call from my father, I had been a broken man. I had been questioning everything. I had lost all faith in myself. But then I got some signals from the lord which told me I was not a total failure. There were rays of hope. I valued my friends and would go to any length for the people I truly cared for. My education as an engineer might have not been a glorious success, but I would never embarrass myself in the journey of life.

"Switch on the computer. There is some news on Aaj Tak," I said urgently.

"What kind of news?" Punit fiddled with the computer.

"Not exactly sure. There is a flash strike all around the market downstairs."

We connected to the internet and the site. A good looking guy wearing a white shirt appeared on the screen.

"… attacks on buses. Shops are being shut down. We hear many are injured though no one has confirmed any deaths. For more details, we will move to our correspondent in Kalyan."

We got the gist that RJS leader Maan Duggad was taken to jail on charges of attacks on north Indian candidates who had come to

Kalyan for appearing in the railway recruitment examinations last Sunday. The violence was the after effect of Maan Duggad's arrest.

It all started after the speech by RJS leader Maan Duggad. He said that north Indians should not be allowed to work in Maharashtra. Most of the high paying designations are captured by north Indians and Maharashtrians have to face unemployment. There was a massive attack on the north Indian candidates at the test centre. A pregnant lady got injured. She was taken to the hospital, but the doctors were not able to save her child. A case of murder had been registered against Maan Duggad, following which he was arrested. The supporters objected to it in the form of this protest.

The screen came alive with the wild, heart-wrenching video of collided vehicles and the road smeared with the blood of innocents.

Punit closed the news window.

"This is ridiculous. I don't believe it," Sahil was angry.

"If north Indians have talent, why can't they get good jobs here?" I asked.

"There is no reservation for Marathi people in Maharashtra while considering jobs," Punit argued.

"Why the hell did he involve innocent students?" Sahil was breathing heavily.

"He has the freedom of speech. He can say whatever he likes," Punit added.

Our discussion trickled to a stop, because we were the common people who sit among the crowd, watch the drama, and don't do anything.

"As far as I remember, your train is at 6 in the evening. Why are you leaving so early?" Punit asked.

"You never know how much time it will take, with the current situation," I picked up my strolley.

I hastened towards the auto stand. I had to reach the railway station as early as possible. I was going to my hometown after many months to celebrate Diwali with my family. Suddenly, I was stopped.

Two men approached in a CD 100 bike, both of them with blue, orange and green turbans with patches of white, tightly wrapped around their heads. The bike stopped in front of a bus. Some people, including a kid and elderly sat inside. Most of the seats were vacant. The man sitting on the backseat of the motorcycle sauntered towards the bus with a thick iron rod in his hand. Before anyone could react, he hit the bus window with the iron rod. With a loud noise, the glass broke into tiny pieces. Most of the pieces scattered inside the bus, while a few scattered on the road. Everyone inside the bus ran towards the door. One of them shouted at the person. However, when you are from a big party with big politicians as your mentors, you don't have to listen to the common people's voices. He gesticulated his rod towards the other windows. Within minutes, the bus was deserted, as if it had stood in that place for years.

The man signalled to the biker. The bike started and before anyone could nab them, they hit the empty roads, leaving behind people in pain.

I ran towards the bus, leaving my strolley. I noticed bleeding faces of those who had not managed to escape. I saw an old uncle in a white kurta-pyjama and a white Nehru cap. He was bleeding from his face. I pulled out my handkerchief and handed it to the old uncle.

"Please take this," I said.

He grabbed the handkerchief with his quivering fingers and said, "*Tujaa aitmaa aabaar* (thanks a lot to you)."

I could not understand a single word. I replied, "I don't understand Marathi."

His expression changed. He pushed back my hand, throwing the kerchief back at me. "Keep your things. We are facing this because of you people."

I couldn't respond. I picked the strolley and trudged to look for a vehicle which could take me to Swargate. I found an auto after some struggle.

On reaching Swargate, I started looking for another auto that could take me to the railway station. There was shattered glass on the road. They spoke of the numerous attacks on buses and other vehicles. I never understood people's behaviour in situations like these.

There were no people on the road. A few animals who didn't know about Indian states and their boundaries and differences between humans of every state were the only ones who walked the roads. The tragic face of that old uncle still haunted me.

I don't know what made me do it. I took my thumb inside my mouth, put it between my upper and lower jaws and bit on it, hard, almost crying with pain. I checked my thumb. The blood that oozed out was similar to the one on uncle's face. I could not find any difference. Same blood ran through my body, as through other Maharashtrians in the state. How could they differentiate then? Maybe, politicians in our country could find a difference between me and a 'Maratha'. I couldn't. I thought about the flying birds and the wind that blew. They were lucky. They could go to any state. They didn't know what a boundary was. What have we earned by being humans?

"Station, sir," the auto rickshaw driver called out.

"Oh!"

I was outside the railway station. I pulled out my luggage from the auto rickshaw and paid the driver. I was going to a different state, a state where there is no difference whether you come from Bengal or Punjab, where before being a Bihari or a Kashmiri we are something else. We all are Indians.

The Farewell

I faced the crowd. They thought I couldn't, so they wanted to hear me. The cacophony, "Viraj, Viraj..." was for them to see me fail, in front of everyone.

It was farewell day. Maybe special for many who sat in that hall. It was not so special for many of us. I stared at their faces. I didn't have words. I looked at people on the desk. Prof Jawrekar, HOD of Computer Engineering Department, Prof Choksey, now HOD of IT Department, and our respected Prof Pawar. Everyone looked at me, expectantly. Prof Pawar gestured me to start.

I looked at the crowd again. There was silence in the hall.

"I was four years old when my father held my small fingers and took me to a big water tank which was under construction. He is a a civil engineer in the Drinking Water and Sanitation Department. That was the day I decided I would become an engineer. Things were different then. I wanted to become a civil engineer. Large buildings and bridges were the most beautiful things that I wanted to construct. Today, I stand in front of you, not as a civil engineer, but as a computer engineering student. Two months and I will be done with all my papers. Anyone among you can say, 'You are an engineer, dude! Will I be happy then?' I asked the crowd.

"Yes..." "Definitely..." "Of course..." and a lot of similar answers popped in chorus.

"I don't feel like an engineer. I never dreamt I would be this kind of an engineer. I am an engineer with no job, poor marks and an engineering degree that came to me in five years. What should I be proud of? What have I gained? I don't have an answer. Then how can I be happy?" I asked the crowd again.

Nobody had an answer.

"Most of my friends left the college last year. Few of them are here among you. A few will take another year to pass out. What is there to be happy about? Two months later, everyone will leave this city. Few may go to their hometown to help their parents in their business, few will go to different cities for jobs. Who will be a friend? Whom will I ask – Dude! Which girl are you dating today, though I already know that you have one girlfriend and the rest are just your good friends?" I looked at Vijay.

"When Nikhil will come after a good shave and a clean bath, will I be able to say – Why didn't you take a bath today? Will he reply – I did take a bath today, ass! Will I be able to respond with – You look like this after taking a bath! How disgusting would you look when you don't? Will we be able to laugh on these comments and repartees?"

The crowd was smiling.

"I don't have an answer, whether engineering did any good to me or not? I don't think so. What it gave me is not something to celebrate or be proud of. Not a thing makes me happy. How or when will I be happy then? Imagine Nikhil sitting in a luxurious chair with a laptop on his desk in his fully air conditioned office, maybe ten years later, with a beautiful secretary in a micro mini skirt scheduling his meetings and Praneet goes to visit him. When they both talk about me for a moment and remember me with a smile on their face,

I will be happy at that moment. Then I will think my engineering journey has been a success. It will be in the truest sense, at that very moment," I paused. I saw Prof Sule smiling at me.

"I apologize to all my professors who asked me not to share my assignments with my friends. I always did. I am really sorry. But ma'am, some teacher had taught me someday when I was a child to help my friends. I was just doing that."

The faculty members smiled.

"Enough of boring you with my lackadaisical speech. Don't worry. I won't take away the job of boring students from our beloved teachers. Kindly allow me to take your leave, and welcome our next speaker. Thanks a lot for all your love and care. I will miss you all," I said and left the dais.

I could see smiles on my faculties' faces and hear hoots from my batch-mates.

After the function, we wrote messages on each other's shirts and left. The memories were captured in rolls of cameras.

A Day Rushing

I was to leave Pune the very next day. After four rounds of interview process at the startup named, Revenue Science, I wasn't selected. Most of my friends had already left the city after the final project submission, while a few, including me, were leaving in a couple of days. I wished to see Nimisha one last time. I had borrowed Punit's bike and was driving towards MG Road, alone.

"Goddamit! You bastard," I yelled at the driver, whose bus almost killed me.

The driver did not bother to stop, continuing to move in the same fashion, as if he had the license to fly an aircraft but was forced to drive a bus instead.

Having lost my balance, I slowed my vehicle, stopping at one of the corners of the road. Before I could normalize my rapid, angry breaths, I witnessed a two wheeler colliding with the bus. As I watched the scattering glass pieces, the female rider was thrown off the scooter.

Spectators surrounded the spot.

I tried to peep, but my eyes could barely manage a few inches before hitting a curious head or another.

I could see bits and pieces of fair skin, now rapidly being coated in bright red blood. The Honda Activa lay on her side. I was disturbed. This was so similar to that day, when I had met that Maharashtrian old man.

My eyes caught a glimpse. Instantly, my limbs froze, and eyes refused to believe what they saw.

Blindly I parked the bike on one corner of the road and rushed towards the crowd, like a man possessed.

I am not sure how many I pushed aside roughly, before my worst fears were confirmed. I had been hoping against hope that I had just imagined it, but there she was. Nimisha lay on the road, unconscious. I had not wanted to meet her in such circumstances.

The blood from her head and right leg was fast trying to find home, spreading far and wide. Hundreds witnessed the accident, but none cared to help.

I moved towards her.

Someone from the crowd called out, "Don't go there. It's a police case."

I couldn't speak, but a voice from deep within me emerged, "Will you let her die on the road?"

I hauled the Activa that entrapped her legs. A few joined me. Lifting her in my arms, I rushed out, breaking and pushing the crowd. A few strangers were by my side. I always wished to hold her in my arms, but had never imagined it would feel like this.

I moved to the nearest vehicle – a shiny dark blue Honda City. I signalled the driver to open the back door. As I got closer, the window rolled down. A gold bangles-adorned hand came out.

"Get away. Are you out of your mind?" the voice of the thickset woman vigorously shaking her hand greeted me, as if the mere touch of Nimisha's breath would contaminate her car.

"Ma'am, she is hurt, we need to go to the nearest hospital. Please help us," I begged her, gesturing her to open the door.

"If you get all that blood on the car seat, Mr Rane will never allow me to take the car. I don't want a dead woman's ghost in my car to haunt me," the woman said and rolled up the window. "Driver, get out of here," were the last words I heard.

Seething, I rushed to an auto rickshaw that had just stopped. A passenger sat in it, luggage by his side.

"Please come out," I said.

"But why? I have hired it," he replied.

"Can't you see? She is dying!" I screamed at the poor man, whose only mistake was that he was out on his own business.

He considered.

Meanwhile, one of the strangers beside me picked up his luggage, saying, "Come out. I will get you another one."

I pushed Nimisha's deadweight inside the auto, got in, and before I could find a spot for me on the seat, asked the driver to move.

"Let me collect his fare," the auto driver responded.

"I will pay you. Move!" I said urgently. Why didn't anyone understand the gravity of the situation? Nimisha was suffering.

"Where?"

"Nearest hospital. Fast!" I urged, resting Nimisha's head on my chest.

She did not respond to my thudding heart.

I took out my handkerchief and placed it on her head in an attempt to stop the heavy blood flow. She continued to bleed. It had been a couple of minutes but my light blue shirt had already turned red. The auto stopped at Bhandari Hospital.

I almost threw a couple of hundred rupee notes at the driver. Gently sliding her out, I carried her in my arms.

I rushed into the building. I pressed the elevator button twice or thrice, the numbers on the display panel blinked sluggishly. The elevator was moving too slowly. I rushed upstairs into the hospital lobby.

A guard tried to stop me, but couldn't. It all happened in fractions of a second.

I crossed the reception on my left, entering a room on the right. There was an empty bed and I placed Nimisha there carefully.

I was soaked in fast drying blood. So was her face, the blood steadily trickling from her head and face. I rushed out, catching hold of a doctor in the next cabin.

"Who allowed you in here?" he inquired as soon as I approached him.

"She is injured," I panted. "Please come. Help her!"

"Can't you see I am attending to a patient here? A hospital has rules," the doctor was annoyed at my unexpected arrival.

My hand itched to get hold of the doctor's collar, but before I could act, I felt a soft pat on my shoulder.

"Where is the injured patient?" asked an old man, his hair chalk white with years of experience.

"Sir, come with me," I said rushing towards Nimisha.

As soon as he saw her, he asked, "Hey, is this Nimisha?" He was unsure due to the mask of caked blood.

"Yes. Do you know her?" I asked amazed.

"His father and I were college friends. We have spent many years together," he explained. "Could you please call the nurse from the room at the end of the lobby?" he instructed politely.

I rushed to the room the doctor had pointed at, returning with the nurse.

"We have to go for an urgent surgery. Move the patient to the OT," the doctor ordered the nurse. He turned to me, "What's your name?"

"Viraj," I said, panting.

"Did you call her parents? We need to take care of formalities before I can start the procedure," the doctor explained.

"No, I was in a rush. What do you need me to do?"

"Call her dad," he said leaving the room.

I looked at Nimisha.

The auto driver had brought her large purse, which I had forgotten in his vehicle. It lay at the foot of the bed. I took out her mobile and looked at the contacts. It took me less than a minute to find 'Dad' in the list.

I dialled the number. Before anyone could answer, I disconnected the call. I could hear my loud heartbeats. Trying to breathe in as much air as possible, I called her dad's number again.

"Hey, why did you disconnect? Have a little patience child. It takes time for old bones to move," the voice on the other end of the phone spoke lovingly.

"Hello," I said haltingly.

"Who are you? Why do you have Nimisha's mobile?" the old man was surprised.

"Nimisha..." I mumbled, "Nimisha has met with an accident," I paused. There was silence.

"Hello... hello..." I enquired.

"How is she?" the voice had changed completely.

"I don't know."

"What do you mean?" There was disbelief. "Where is she?"

"In the OT. There was a lot of blood. Her head, leg, face..." I trailed as the images flashed past my eyes.

"Where are you? Which hospital?"

"I am at Bhandari Hospital."

The call was disconnected.

I thought of calling him again. I doubted he would be able to cope with the situation so I decided to wait for a while.

The old doctor was speaking to someone on the phone in the hall. As soon as the doctor's call ended, Nimisha's mobile rang. It said, 'Dad calling'.

"I spoke to Dr Rajiv Bhandari. He will do his best. I will reach Pune as soon as possible. Meanwhile, could you just stay with her? Please...for a while, could you take care of my baby for me? Let me know the situation from time to time...please?"

"Yes Uncle," I assured him. I don't know during which part of his instructions my eyes had brimmed. They were flowing now, uninhibited.

I sat on the sofa in the hall, closed my eyes and whispered to god.

"God, if ever I have done anything good in my entire life, please save her. Give her life back, and I promise I shall worship you all my life, with no more expectations from you…"

Before I could end my prayers, Nimisha's phone rang, again. It was her dad.

"Can I have your number?"

I gave it to him.

I closed my eyes again and started to pray.

"Yes, you?" The nurse's voice made me open my eyes. I saw her pointing at me.

I walked up to her.

"Take this prescription. Get the medicines and injections from the medical store downstairs," she placed a slip in my palm.

I took the slip and walked downstairs.

I don't know how many hours passed. The red bulb outside the OT still glowed. The red bulb seemed to have a power. Bad thoughts churned in my mind, but I tried to push them away. I told myself, *She is a very nice girl. God won't do anything wrong to her. She will be alright.*

The bulb lost its glow and the OT door finally opened. Dr Bhandari stepped out and I ran towards him.

"How is she?"

"She is still unconscious. Her condition is a little better than when you brought her. Though, I am afraid, she is not completely out of danger. I can't predict her exact condition until we get the X-ray reports. She also has blood clots in some section of her brain," he paused for breath.

"Okay." My heartbeat had calmed but I was still worried.

I called up her dad, though it was quite late in the night. I gave him all the necessary details. It was really difficult for me. But thinking about her father, I tried to stay calm. He told me he was at the airport and would be reaching Pune in the morning.

It would be difficult for one of the leading surgeons of the country, from AIIMS, to say to another doctor, "Please save my daughter."

I walked to the OT peeping through the small glass, trying to see her. Scared. It is not every day you stand outside an OT, looking at the pale face of the girl who had redefined your life.

"Can you move away? We have to transfer the patient for an X-ray," a nurse ordered from behind.

I removed myself from the front of the door. The ward boy moved towards her with a stretcher. I went to the hall, steeling myself to look at her.

My heartbeats got louder, again.

The phone started vibrating. I moved my hands absently, searching for it.

"Hey! Where have you been, man?" Punit enquired.

"Shit! I really forgot about your bike. Could you please come to Bhandari Hospital? I will return the keys," I said.

"Hospital? Is everything alright?" Punit asked, concerned.

"Please come. I will explain," I said and disconnected.

I went to the X-ray room. A nurse stopped me at the entrance but I didn't listen to her.

I started walking towards Nimisha's stretcher. I could not feel anything. I heard the nurse asking me questions. A strong hold gripped my hand, and I could not move. My lifeless eyes rested on Nimisha's bandaged body.

The guard held me, ordered by the nurse to stop me. I struggled with the guard. I noticed he was the same guy who had stopped me earlier. The forced silence of the place was pierced by our commotion and Dr Bhandari came out.

"Look. If you shout anymore in my hospital, I will have to get you thrown out. What do you want?" he asked.

"I just want to see her." A teardrop rolled down my right cheek.

Dr Bhandari instructed the guard to leave my hand, "We are shifting her to the ward. You can't see her in the X-ray room."

I saw her finally, after a couple of hours.

Her face was still innocent, but bandaged. The right eyebrow seemed to have disappeared. The lips dried, bloodless. My heart wept at her condition. A thick tube ran up her nose, and disappeared deep inside her. The right arm had turned green, due to the many IVs piercing her body.

Medicines lay on a corner table, not far from large steel masses, with monitors surrounding her on all sides. A small monitor with small curves beside her measured her heart beat. An oxygen cylinder tube skirted past it to cover her mouth and nose. I was shaken. I could not see her in this condition. I nearly ran out of the room.

Punit had arrived. I recounted the accident, returning his bike's keys. I told him of the place where he would find his bike, parked next to the corner street light.

He offered to stay there, asked me to have something to eat. I refused. He left but came back with a food packet and forced me to eat.

I opened the packet, and was about to take the first bite of a chapati, when a voice spoke, "Hey Viraj, did you get in touch with her colleagues and friends?" Dr Bhandari asked.

"No sir. I don't know them."

"Nimisha has lost a lot of blood. We need donors. Attendants, family members, anyone who could help her," he continued, spreading his hand in a helpless gesture. "We could not get certified blood from the blood bank."

"I will donate my blood, as much as you want," I said after thinking for a moment.

That was the day I came to know why god sent me to earth with O+ blood group. It was for this critical moment.

"No. Not you. You are the only one here to take care of her. I'm not sure her father can arrive before tonight. Ask any of her colleagues from office or her neighbours. Can you? We are running out of time."

"I will. I can manage taking care of her after giving blood," I assured the doctor.

"What's her blood group, doctor?" Punit asked.

"It's B+."

What can a person with an A+ blood group say after that? Punit's blood was not required.

Considering Nimisha's critical condition, the doctor asked me to follow him.

I was taken to lab for initial tests. Thankfully, my blood matched the requirements.

The doctor suggested I should eat before donating. I gulped the food Punit had brought, in record speed.

I went inside the room.

I lay down on a bed. She lay beside me. A tube ran through my left hand to a bottle that was tied to the metal frame at the top.

Another pipe emerged from the bottle, and entered her right arm. Drops of blood came via the pipe in my left hand, and started trickling into the bottle. I could clearly hear each drop, as it filled the bottle. It took almost an hour.

The nurse closed the notch of the pipe on my hand, and removed the IV.

"That will be all," she confirmed.

Few minutes later, she came with a glass of orange juice in her hand.

"You can go out now," she said moving towards the stretcher.

The blood started its outflow from the bottle. The drops slowly travelling the pipe that disappeared into Nimisha's arm.

I felt a little relaxed, so walked out of the room.

"You must go to your room. I will stay here. Come in the morning," Punit instructed me when the nurse said only one of the attendants could stay in the hospital.

"No buddy, you go. You have your office in the morning. It's already late."

"You are right. Don't worry. Call if you need anything," Punit assured me.

"It's okay. I will call if required. I was to travel home tomorrow. If I need to cancel the tickets, I will let you know. Thanks for coming."

Punit left.

The dark night surrounded the hospital. Nimisha was again moved to a different room. The doctors said they would check her condition the next morning. I sat near her on a chair, staring.

Her injuries had changed her a lot.

She was not as beautiful as she used to be. But I still loved her, in spite of the cuts on her face, no eyebrows and her damaged right leg.

I tried to memorize the scars she got that day.

I don't remember when I fell asleep.

"Get up. It's late," a nurse said pushing the window curtains aside. The sun glared on my face.

I looked at my watch. It said, 9:12 a.m.

"How long was I sleeping? Why didn't you wake me before this?" I asked the nurse.

"You were the last person to sleep in the hospital. The nurse informed me an hour ago, before she left."

"Good morning, Viraj. How are you?" Dr Bhandari greeted me as soon as he entered the room.

"Good morning. I am fine."

"You will be glad to know that the reports say the blood clots in her brain are minor. It can heal with the right medication. Hopefully, she will wake up in a few hours. You will be able to talk to her," he added.

"Thank you, doctor. Thanks for everything you did." I hugged him tightly.

"I did my duty. That's all. I think your contribution really helped her. Thanks to you for saving my friend's daughter," he said patting my shoulder.

I felt relieved as I glanced at her.

A while later, her parents entered the hospital. She had not woken up till then.

"I need to leave now," I said to her father as he came inside the room.

"I don't know how to thank you son, for everything you did for her," her father said.

"It was my duty."

"When will you come back?" he inquired.

"I have to catch a train to my hometown. I haven't even packed my luggage yet. I haven't had breakfast either." My stomach grumbled, as if on cue. "I have to clean my teeth too," I tried to smile, showing my teeth to him.

He hugged me close to his heart and said, "Thank you, beta."

I greeted Nimisha's mother, reassuring her.

It was time to leave the room. I glanced at her for the last time. Her father held her fingers, she tried to hold it back with her weaker ones.

She was coming out of her unconsciousness.

I could not stop a teardrop that made its way out of my left eye.

I touched her mother's feet, walked out of the room and finally out of the hospital.

I did not look back.

Epilogue

Six months later

The mobile rang repeatedly. I unlocked my washroom and rushed to my phone. The number was familiar. However, I could not place it.

"Hello," I took the call.

"Are you stupid?" a sweet voice asked.

I was confused. Who the hell had called me to ask if I was stupid?

"Couldn't you share your number? The least you could have done is left it with my dad. None of our classmates have it. Where did you vanish? Nobody knows where you are." Questions were fired without a pause.

I knew that voice. It was the voice my ears always wanted to hear. All I could do was speak her name, "Nimisha."

"So, you remember me?"

"You think I can forget the best thing that ever happened to me?" I was slowly coming out of the initial shock.

"Then, why didn't you call me?"

"You asked me not to."

"You are crazy as well."

"Yeah, I am mad." I grinned. "Mad about you."

"Okay. Are you free next week?" she asked giggling on the other end.

"What do you mean?"

"Will you be able to meet me next week?"

"Umm... Oo..." I hemmed and hawed.

"Tell me," she asked, slowly.

"I can die for that single day."

"You don't have to die. Just arrange for my accommodation. I will be coming to see you, honey."

"*Sacchi?*"

"*Muchi.*"

"I can do that."

"I am going to the US next month with my colleagues. I want to see you before that," she lowered her voice.

"Don't worry, I will. For sure."

"Bye," she said.

"Bye."

"Hey, if you want, we can be good friends," she said and giggled.

"We will be," I said.

She disconnected the phone.

I am really happy. She is coming this week to visit me. By the way, I shifted to Bangalore and am working with a startup. It is a respectable job, with a lot of responsibilities.

I scored an unbelievable 72.43% marks in my last semester with a forty in just a single paper. I believe 37 + grace marks still works for me. Punit is with an MNC in Gurgaon and has bought an i10. He assured me, he will take me for a drive when I visit him.

Sahil left engineering after trying for a few extended years. He went to his hometown and joined some open state university to pursue B.C.A. Open state university is basically an open book state university where he can open his books to copy his answers. He just has to make notes of the page numbers where the answers can be found a day prior to his exams. He will be completing his graduation this year.

Laila fell in love with Sohail. They seem to be going strong on Facebook. Last seen, she posted her pictures with him playing Ludo together.

Sometimes, I believe, the almighty sitting up there is also a big fan of Bollywood movies, because at the end of the story, he makes everything perfect. Like after small drops of unseasonal rain comes lovely sunshine. Like after a heavy meal comes sweet dessert. But the dessert's flavour depends on how we have our meal. I guess I have learnt to eat the meal. It was finally time to enjoy some dessert.